HEALING TOUCH

DESTINATION LOST BOOK 1

MISSY WELSH

ABOUT THIS BOOK

A routine mission from the Moon Colony to Earth ends in the five-man crew of the Swallowtail being transported to the other side of the galaxy. Met with hostility, captured, and tortured simply for being Human, the three survivors hold little hope for their futures.

Captain Noah O'Keefe has lost his ship and his crew to alien forces he didn't even know existed until a few hours ago. Chemically blinded and helpless, he can only rely on the kindness of strangers to escape a dungeon and try to recover what he's lost.

Vivek Korraay has the fate of the universe in his hands, but around every corner is another crisis...or a blue-eyed Human whose needs he cannot ignore. Spying has lost its appeal and Vivek longs for a simpler life and someone to share it with.

Can Noah and Vivek survive pursuit on land and in space long enough to prevent a war?

And, if they do, might a true and binding love be their reward?

CHAPTER ONE

UNKNOWN SPACE

Dying in outer space had always been a possibility for a Moon Colony drop-ship captain like Noah O'Keefe.

Equipment malfunctions, fatal injuries, and the rare explosion took lives every now and then. *Never knew when your number might be up.* Anyone in this line of work could be here and gone in an instant.

But he'd thought he had plenty of time anyway. Settle down, get married, raise a family, and maybe even do all that on the moon...someday. No reason to contemplate his own death like an approaching deadline. No reason to rush anything.

He never thought he'd have *months* to think about dying. Dying right here in *Swallowtail's* dimly lit cockpit with its useless navigational system endlessly flashing *Error: Destination Lost.*

Noah pressed a fist to his chest, trying to stem the ache there. Maybe the stress would kill him before the battery cells drained completely or they ran out of water.

Just one last trip... Goddamn. He closed his eyes and tried for deep breaths. Aviary Corporation had probably already told their families the five of them were dead. *These things happen. Sorry for your loss.*

After three months of slowly going insane with worry, he'd decided to push the ship toward a nearby planet. Price, the engineer they'd been transporting, had rigged up a probe to punch through the atmosphere in the hope the planet's blue water and green land masses were a sign they might survive there. They were still waiting for a report from the damn thing ten hours later.

And now the hope was killing him. *Killing him...*

His great-grandfather's dagger sat on the useless console in front of him. He stared at it gleaming in its custom cherry wood case inlaid with the family crest. He wouldn't go out gasping, shivering, or delirious. He'd choose his own fate.

When the time came.

"Noah?"

He snapped the case shut, waited a heartbeat for a comment. When none came, he turned toward his pilot.

Ledger Atwater's pale face showed the strain of being lost in space for ninety-four days. His blue eyes were red-rimmed and bruised. He had let his long, black hair down to hang past his shoulders, but unlike Noah he'd kept shaving his face. He wore a dingy, sleeveless T-shirt, boxers, and socks, his uniform nowhere in sight.

"The probe's sending back some info." Ledger offered a weary smile. "It sounds pretty good."

Noah took a deep breath. That ache in his chest eased a bit. "Finally."

He guided himself from his seat. As Ledger floated away, Noah tucked the dagger's case under the console. Slowly, he sailed along behind Ledger into the next compartment.

Price had reprogrammed the robot inside the probe to take atmospheric and soil readings, plus seek out and analyze water sources. Like the rest of them, Noah had prayed.

Ledger hooked an arm through a loop near the round doorway. Noah did the same beside Barstow, who was some kind of plant scientist. Price stood near the monitors, his eyes actively scanning the scrolling report. Dunkirk, the Aviary Corporation suit, hovered nearby, nibbling on his thumbnail. It was amazing he hand any nails left to bite.

"Ledger says you might have good news," Noah said. Three frowning faces looked over at him. "Is he wrong?"

"Well, no," Price said and scratched at his unshaven cheek.

Even with just two words, his sexy Texas twang was evident. Once upon a time, Noah had thought they might... But no, nothing other than survival mattered now.

"It's not Earth," Price went on, "but it's not bad. Not bad at all."

"We could survive there," Barstow said. "Theoretically, anyway."

Even in a crisis situation, Barstow's inability to commit to anything came shining through. Whining and prone to hypochondria, he was Noah's least favorite person on this mission. *We'll eat him first.* Noah nearly laughed aloud.

Ledger's voice crackled with irritation as he snapped, "As theoretical as that wormhole that zapped us out here, Barstow?"

Barstow bristled. "That wasn't *my* fault."

"*Hey,*" Noah said. "We're not going there again." He stared at Ledger until he ducked his head behind his hair with a minute nod.

On their return trip, just about halfway between Earth and the moon, a once-theoretical Einstein-Rosen Bridge had appeared out of nowhere and sucked them in. Like traveling through the middle of a straw, *Swallowtail* went in one end and popped out the other several hours later. And the other side of the straw could be anywhere in the universe for all they knew. Without the connection to Earth, they were flying blind.

Noah looked to Barstow again. "How's the soil? Could we plant those seedlings?"

Behind a glass window set into the wall, a myriad collection of young, edible plants sat in groups. They might be all that stood between five people and starvation in the terrifyingly near future.

"Yes, I think so," Barstow said while his brown eyes flicked all over the results on the screen in front of him. "The conditions of the planet's soil would indicate that it's full of... That it's *very* fertile."

"Air? Water?" Noah asked. "It's all good?"

"Oxygen content's a little high," Barstow said continued. "If Earth was the city, this is the country. Hardly any pollutants, and those could be natural. The water's salt-free and cold, so I'd guess the probe found a freshwater stream."

"I say we take our chances there." Price leaned on the counter in front of him, his feet hooked into loops that let him stay where he was. "We already know what'll happen if we don't go down."

Dunkirk spoke up. "We have to make sure the ship continues to emit a signal, so Aviary will be able to find us." The pretty, little man refused to believe the company had given up on them.

Everyone looked to Noah. Ledger did because he was trained to, and the rest because it was his job to see to their safety. While he took his job very seriously, he'd never imagined it would include colonization.

"Ledger, set course. Let's get—"

A constant, high-pitched beeping cut him off.

"What is that?"

"What's happening?"

"Are we crashing?"

Noah dove through the doorway, toward the controls. What he saw through the cockpit windows froze the breath in his lungs.

The entire front view was blocked by a wall of smooth, dark gray metal panels surrounding what could only be a landing bay. It was ringed in blue light and illuminated within, letting Noah see several bullet-shaped ships and...huge snakes?

Oh, shit.

CHAPTER TWO

As *Swallowtail* passed through the opening into the bay, gravity returned, slamming them all to the floor. Noah smacked his chin on the headrest of his chair before ending up on his hands and knees behind it. "Fuck," he said, his whole body aching. He grunted as he hauled himself up.

When he was finally on his feet, the transport touched down on the floor of the landing bay, nearly knocking him back to his knees. He stumbled toward the locker beside the hatch as enormous snake-monsters swarmed outside the window. *Don't think about it. Just get your weapon.*

Dunkirk screamed, Price and Barstow yelled curses, but Noah concentrated on punching his code into the locker's panel. Inside were their e-pistols.

The "zap guns" shot a gluey, metallic bullet that could carry an electrical charge from twelve to fifty amps. When it hit, it adhered to the skin of its victim and released the charge. Noah had used his to subdue an angry drunk once. His hand shook as he set it.

"Full charge," he told Ledger.

Ledger looked at him for a moment, and then retrieved his own gun.

"I'm not taking chances," Noah said. "If they're friendly, fine. If not, I want as much punch as possible." What they'd do after that, he couldn't think about now.

A huge sword sliced into *Swallowtail's* hull.

Noah and Ledger shoved the others out of the way and took their stand opposite the sword. *A sword? Seriously?* The damn thing sliced through the hull as if it was nothing more than tin foil. Three green, clawed fingers grabbed hold of the top of the cut section and pulled it down. Noah shot as soon as he saw exposed skin. The alien snake fell back, shaking with the electrical surge from its arrow-shaped head to the pointed tip of its tail.

Another one took its place, and Ledger shot it. Though his bullet hit a furred sash crossing the snake's lean chest, when it reached up to brush the goo away, the contact with its fingers gave it the shock.

When another alien slithered up, Noah tried to shoot, but his gun wouldn't fire. He tried to push the lever down, get a lower charge, but it wouldn't let him. He'd never had to shoot more than one at a time, and never at this level. The damn thing hadn't had time to recharge itself.

A sword come through another wall, right into Price.

Noah froze. Price touched the bloody blade, a sick kind of surprise on his face. The sword was withdrawn, and Price collapsed to the floor like a broken doll. As Noah continued to watch in stunned horror, Dunkirk knelt down by Price and checked for vitals.

"Oh, god," Dunkirk said as he stood back up. "Oh, *god.*"

Noah's gun beeped with a full charge. He startled, raised his arm. One of those monsters slapped the gun from his hand, shoved him to the floor. They were so damn *fast*. One of the aliens clamped a hand on the back of his neck and lifted him. He yelled in pain.

The snake-monster slammed him face-first against the wall beside the missing section and leaned an arm on him. Noah tried to push off the wall, but the fucker leaned harder. Noah gave in when he could barely draw a breath.

Outside in the bay, Ledger was face down on the ground, his hands bound behind him. The snake pinning Noah fastened his hands together now, and he didn't resist. It shoved him out into the bay area. With a fist in Dunkirk's hair, another snake brought him out. Noah heard Barstow hollering moments before he came stumbling out, landing on his knees beside Dunkirk.

An snake came out of *Swallowtail* and threw Price's body down at Noah's feet.

He needed to close those green eyes. Death had taken Price so fast he looked frozen in shock. He was gone, Noah knew that, *believed* that, but it didn't seem final with Price's dead eyes staring up at him.

A snake-monster hissed at Barstow. He scrambled to his feet and crashed into Noah.

"Get a *grip*," he said as another snake slithered

toward them. "Just do what they want, and we might get out of this alive." He shoved Barstow away with his shoulder, but all the man did was drop back to his knees and start wailing.

An alien thrust its sword into the back of Barstow's neck.

"No!"

Rage and horror tore out of Noah as he yelled wordlessly. These were his people! They couldn't be *captured* like this. *Killed* like this.

Not without a fight.

Noah looked around desperately until he saw Ledger's gun was only a few feet away from them. Most of the aliens stood around talking to each other, none near enough to interfere and, apparently, feeling like the humans weren't worth worrying about. Noah caught Ledger's eye and nodded toward the zap gun. Ledger stared back with wide eyes.

"Six-six-nine-six-four-five," Noah shouted, hoping his own zap gun inside *Swallowtail* would pick up the command code. When a red light began flashing on the grip of Ledger's gun, Noah gave the final command. "Self-destruct, twenty seconds!"

While the light blinked off the seconds, Ledger lifted his leg to kick the gun away. As soon as he moved, though, one of the aliens barked and started toward him. Ledger backed up.

Frustration added to the boil of Noah's rage. He ran over and kicked the gun himself, sending it under a ship near the cluster of aliens. Designed to make sure competitors couldn't get ahold of proprietary technology, the zap gun self-destruct would not just explode but give off an electromagnetic pulse, too. Noah smiled just before the impact knocked him on his ass.

A klaxon started up, the lights flickered, and Dunkirk was screaming again. Noah watched *Swallowtail* burn and listened to alien chaos. He struggled back up to his feet. It was possible he'd just taken out a few of the aliens.

One of them grabbed Noah by the front of his flight suit. Noah looked defiantly up into beady, dark eyes.

It had scaled black skin on its back that gradated to bright red down the center of its front. The triangular head had a hood of smaller red scales framing it. A black, forked tongue flicked out at him and long, ivory fangs gleamed. It was definitely a snake, but it had shoulders, arms, and fingers like some kind of horrible genetic experiment.

Noah tried to hold onto his rage, but this was one frightening son of a bitch.

Another one barked, and this one let him go. It swung around to face an alien wearing a thick furred sash like the one Ledger had zapped. Shaking its head, the new one stared at Noah and said, "Ooman."

Noah staggered back. It knew what he was?

The sashed bastard smiled like Noah was amusing. Fucking *smiled*. Noah opened his mouth to tell it off, but something pricked his neck. He spun around.

Another alien stood behind him, grinning. Noah swayed, bracing his legs apart and blinking hard. This was a different kind of alien. It looked like a lion, like a lion-man, and cocked its golden head at him. It was just too surreal, too insane. Snake aliens? Lion aliens? *What the fuck is happening?* Noah stumbled away from it, seeking his crew, something normal. Anything real.

He knew he'd been drugged, but didn't know what to do. What was he supposed to do? He hit the floor with his chest and the side of his face. He had to do some—

CHAPTER THREE

ULVAR FORTRESS

Vivek Korraay calmly lounged in a corner behind the balcony's short wall above King Solong's private chambers. Several risings ago, he had snuck up to this place and hid himself. Beneath a black cloak, he carefully stretched his back muscles as he waited for yet another tap to connect. And, of course, he had to intercept it without the new ruler-for-life below him knowing he was even in the room.

The United Coalition of Planets had secretly sworn to prevent the melding of two hostile peoples, the Golson and these, the Tevian—one a well-armed and organized military presence and the other full to overflowing with blood-thirsty minions. But to prevent it, they needed the date and location of the face-to-face negotiation meeting. Thanks to the high level security of the king's private communication system—one of very few modern conveniences in this ancient stone castle—that information was impossible to gain without someone on the inside. Someone no one would ever suspect, like a healer with a knack for espionage.

Vivek's pulse kicked up when he saw the person who appeared on the screen as the tap connected. This might be the break he had been waiting for. It was a Krittikan, one still proudly bound to Golson rule given the pendant he wore. This had to be about the alliance negotiations.

"Greetings, ruler of Ulvar," the aging Krittikan said via a computerized voice translating Kretch into Tok. "I trust this is finally the tap to arrange our meeting?"

Like all Krittikan, this one was covered in short fur and had a mane of long, thick hair. His had several chins beneath his short snout and his every feature was varying shades of gray. His large golden eyes with their vertically slit pupils were partially hidden by an overlarge brow ridge.

"It is, Official Yuric," King Solong said, his voice unusually pleasant. "How soon can one of your ships arrive?"

Yuric looked startled for a moment, then he focused his attention on someone else in the room with him. Vivek assumed he had expected Solong to come to him, the serf to the lord. Solong's egotism would see it the other way around. They were joining with him.

"My ship could be near Tev in eight turns," Yuric finally said. "We may negotiate the terms of our alliance then."

Vivek smiled. With two brief sentences his mission was complete. After three phases on this desolate, sun-dried planet doing little more than hiding like this, he could leave at last. As soon as he passed on this information, he could go home to Aguada and lose himself in the waters. Be nothing more than a normal male, a gifted healer, no longer under contract to the Coalition's Intelligence Retrieval Bureau.

"Excellent. We will meet aboard your ship." Solong reached for the disconnection switch.

"Ah, yes, I—" Yuric began before Solong cut transmission.

Vivek remained where he was. He would not attempt to leave until Solong was away inspecting the renovations to his throne room, as per his usual schedule. The peace of his mission's end washed through Vivek to the point where he barely felt the stones under him anymore.

Solong's computer suddenly announced that someone was requesting to establish a tap. Vivek kept his interceptor active. A high level Tevian guard appeared on the screen, his furred sash proclaiming his rank.

After an informal greeting to Solong—probably making him a family member—he said, "We encountered a small Human vessel on our return from Trizeylia. I thought—"

"Get rid of them," Solong interrupted with a dismissive wave of his hand. "I care not for their kind. They are too weak and prone to leaking."

Vivek silently cursed, his peace vanishing. He did not need to deal with Humans now that his mission was complete. All he had to do was retrieve his supplies, dig up his ship, and fly into Coalition space to relay his findings. He did not need any possible complications that would come from rescuing innocents.

"These are different from the others we have seen,"

the guard insisted. "They managed to kill two of us before we were able to remove them from their ship."

"How could they do that?" Solong asked incredulously. "They have no defenses."

The Tevian had slightly curved scales to shield them. Killing them either required a great deal of stamina to deliver enough blows, or extremely accurate aim and high velocity. Yet another reason no one wanted them joining an interstellar conflict.

Humans, though, were fantastically delicate and not nearly smart enough to keep themselves from harm on their own planet, let alone out in the rest of the universe. Everything Vivek knew about them depicted them as helpless, ignorant, and easily overpowered. He should abandon them to their fates, but he had seen what Solong liked to do to the weak. Forgetting that much bloody torture was not possible. Vivek could not ignore this.

"It was most interesting," the guard said with obvious excitement to have his leader's attention. "They have weapons that emit a strange sticky substance that delivers an electrical charge to the victim. My soldiers died very quickly."

"I want this weapon," Solong said, a smile in his voice.

He looked concerned. "The weapons have been destroyed, as well as their ship, one of ours, and two guards."

Solong waved it away, and Vivek wondered why he did not go into a rage, as per usual. Instead, he asked, "What have you done with the Humans?"

"One was killed while we were cutting into their ship

—a most weak vessel—and another was killed afterward to end its noise-making." He shrugged dismissively. "There are two others and a Sah'dre male."

Vivek closed his eyes and sighed, both with regret for the lives lost and the fact his ship didn't have room or supplies for four people. One or two he could have taken with him, but not all of them. If the opportunity came where he could still rescue some, he would do so. It was his only option now.

"One of the Humans is remarkably brave," the guard continued. "I believe it is a male. We used *krikti* to subdue him. I thought perhaps you would enjoy making sport with him."

Solong chuckled, making Vivek cringe. "Yes, excellent." Solong's glee was evident. "Bring him here. You said there were others?"

"Another Human, yes. It leaks from its eyes and groin a great deal, but is quiet at least."

Solong grunted as if disappointed. "What is your location?"

"We are nearing the Hyfonda Portal. We should be home in two risings."

"Excellent. Sell the Human and Sah'dre at the portal. If none want them, kill them." Solong smiled hideously. "Bring the brave Human to me. I will extract the secrets of this new weapon from it."

Vivek switched off his interceptor while they spoke on family business, oblivious to the lives they had just decided to destroy. Though the Human would add only complications to his plans, he would still rescue him. He had been unable to heal the last to suffer one of Solong's extractions.

But what had a small ship of Humans been doing here anyway? As far as he knew, they had never managed to leave their own solar system on their own. And why had one of the Sah'dre been with them? Everyone knew not to approach Earth yet.

CHAPTER FOUR

ALIEN SHIP

"Noah? Noah, please wake up."

Holy fuck... My head...

"Noah, are you okay? Can you hear me?"

The voice shaky and desperate, that was Dunkirk—what was his first name? Chris? No, something cuter. Charlie? That was it, Charlie Dunkirk. Kind of a wimpy and nervous little nerd. Pretty face, though. He wouldn't make it.

Noah tried to open his eyes, but, like a hangover from the brightest depths of hell, light made the pain in his head worse. Keeping his eyes closed, he opened his mouth, gagged on the deathly taste, and moaned involuntarily.

"Captain O'Keefe, talk to me," Ledger said, his voice hard. "Come on."

The need to communicate to his crew outweighed any pain.

"Here," he said with a croak. "I'm here." He managed to reach out to them through the excruciating pain in his arm, but no one touched him. Were they separated somehow? Restrained while he was not?

They expressed their thanksgiving while he rolled from his side to his back and slowly straightened out his legs. His muscles felt weak, cramped, as if he'd run too far through sand. His arms felt the same punishment and his back cracked when he finally lay flat. This was way more than the usual gravity deprivation.

They were still talking. "What?" he said.

"How are you?" Ledger asked.

Noah nodded, his eyes closed. "Fucked up."

"They injected you with something. You were out cold in seconds."

Dunkirk asked with concern, "Are you sure you're—"

Noah didn't want to hear it. "Where are we?"

"Some kind of holding block," Ledger answered. "Rows of cells with bars on the doors. I'm across from yours and Dunkirk's on your right."

"Are we alone?"

"No," Dunkirk spoke up, sounding calmer, in control. "I counted six physically different aliens in separate cells. None of them speak any of the languages Ledger and I know." He paused, then said mournfully, "Which doesn't surprise me since they're all *Earth* languages."

Noah swore when he tried to open his eyes again, but the pain and weakness of his limbs was fading. In the moments of silence, he became aware of a quiet discussion among the other people near them. A language of clicks dominated with a Russian-sounding one beneath it. Visions of movie aliens flashed through his throbbing mind. *Any little green men?*

"Are you feeling better?" Dunkirk asked.

"No. Have they said what they want?" Noah tried to sit up and found he could if he leaned against the wall.

Ledger answered. "Nobody's been down here since they left us. And speak of the devil..."

"What?"

"No! Fuck you, I'm *not leaving.*" That was Ledger.

Then Dunkirk, "*No.* No!"

"What's happening?" Noah demanded and got on his knees, trying to find the doorway. Maybe they hadn't closed his cell door because he'd been unconscious. He opened his eyes, but quickly shut them again, the painful whiteness too much to handle on top of still aching muscles. All he could feel around him was smooth metal, no bars, no openings.

"They've cuffed me and— Fuck!" Ledger hollered. "Shackles, too. You son of a bitch!"

"What *is* that?" Dunkirk practically screamed.

"Goddamnit." Noah uselessly felt his way along the wall. He couldn't help them!

"This green centaur thing is taking me away. *Noah!*"

Completely blind, unable to assist in anyway, Noah went with the only thing he could think of and offered that. "Ledger, just go with him. Don't fight!"

"*Don't* fight?" He sounded close to panic.

"I can't *see.* Don't fight them. Don't give them a reason to *blind you.*"

Dunkirk was crying, and Ledger was quiet now. Noah couldn't hear footsteps or rattling chains or anything else to tell him what was happening. His whole body shook with fear and frustration and anger. He was so fucking helpless!

Suddenly, Dunkirk screamed, "They're taking me, too!"

"Don't fight, Charlie. Don't resist. Just be strong. I promise I'll find you. I'll get you *home*."

He couldn't hear if Dunkirk replied to his lies.

For a long time, all Noah heard were the aliens around him talking or shuffling around. Slithering. He fought back panic; it wouldn't do him any good. He made himself sit down again since he couldn't find the damn door and it wasn't like he could go anywhere if he did. He needed to stay smart if he was going to have a hope in hell of making it.

Suddenly, everything started vibrating. It grew steadily more intense until Noah found himself bracing his back against the wall with his knees bent and his arms out to his sides. His muscles protested being tensed and his teeth clicked together even though he clenched his jaw.

Gradually, the vibrating subsided. He remembered the feeling; it was the same as when *Swallowtail* had been inside the wormhole. The horrible shaking happened as they entered and this was while they were inside it. Noah held his head in his hands and leaned over on his knees.

What the hell was he supposed to do?

CHAPTER FIVE

ALIEN PLANET

It was official, he was blind.

That bright whiteness Noah had seen before had darkened to black nothingness.

He was numb. His mind, not his body because he'd obeyed the tugs on his arms to get him up out of his cell and he'd walked where they wanted him to go. He hadn't resisted when he'd been pushed down on a grated floor and kicked until he curled up, hugging his knees to his chest and covering his head. People—*aliens*—had walked by in both directions, something on wheels rolled to a stop beside him, and he just sat. What else could he do?

He felt pretty sure he was on something smaller, his imagination putting him in the rickety training ship they'd used at the Aviary Academy. It had vibrated like it meant to fall apart, too. He wasn't praying to make it safely home this time. Though they were landing, he couldn't even fool himself into believing he was anywhere near Earth.

The shuttle thumped, like maybe they'd landed, and

he heard a machine hum. A sudden blast of desert heat crashed over him, taking his breath away. Yeah, they'd landed...in hell.

One of the aliens grabbed him, hauling him to his feet. Although his hands were unbound, he didn't struggle. Where could a blind man go? It steered him down a ramp into what sounded like a whole crowd of aliens.

Noah stiffened, his blood pounding painfully in his head. A tug at the leg of his flight suit. A poke in his side. He fisted his free hand and swung it back and forth in front of him. Suddenly, the alien barked loudly several times. Murmurs. *Slithering.* The alien picked up its pace, and Noah had no choice but to stumble along beside it. He didn't want to be grateful for the intervention, but he was.

The sun's heat unexpectedly abated. They must have gone inside. He swallowed, knowing he had to concentrate on what he heard. Maybe he could remember the way out by the sounds if he ever got the chance to escape. Once his sight came back. If it did.

Don't panic. Don't you fucking panic.

The floor was sand or loose, dry dirt from the sound of their footsteps. He focused, calmed. He heard the crackling of fire, torches maybe, so he reasoned that he was somewhere dark. Dark, cold, and damp with dirt floors sounded like a dungeon. *Shit. Oh, shit.*

The alien stopped abruptly, jerking him to a halt. Rusty hinges protested. "No," he said. "No!"

He struggled, but he was no match for the alien's brutal shove.

Noah stumbled forward and tripped, crying out when his knees hit the gritty stone floor. He heard the door close with a squeal and a heavy thud behind him. He knelt there, gasping, trying to listen. Was he alone? The only sounds—dripping water, shuffling feet, a sneeze —came from behind him, toward the door. He was alone.

You are not alone.

Noah flinched, holding his hands out as he got to his feet. "Who's there?"

I am Bendel.

He shivered as he realized he wasn't hearing the voice with his ears.

"Am I losing my mind?"

You are gaining mine. The voice was quiet and childlike. *I will help you escape, if you take me with you.*

"I can't see."

You will not need eyes to see what I can show you.

Suddenly, Noah saw the room. It looked like he was peering through the end of a long glass bottle; he could see blurred shapes along the edges of a tunnel with a slightly distorted, round picture at the end. But now he could see each stone wall, patch of alien filth, and thick metal bar. There was a tiny window high up near the ceiling that let a beam of sunlight stab into the gloom. He turned toward the door.

When he enters, run.

"What?" He jerked when he heard plodding footsteps.

The guttural language of his alien captors sent him running toward the dark corner on the same wall as the door. It opened with a squeal and one long snake slithered inside. Another wearing purple cloth and clear jewels was right behind him. They moved farther into the room, heads swiveling, tongue darting—looking for him.

Run, now!

Noah didn't hesitate. Sprinting around the door and into the torch-lit corridor he ran, the voice telling him which way to go. Right down this hall. Left down that one. He ran up two separate flights of stairs. He could hear the snake-monsters yelling behind him as he ran down halls of cells, strange sounds and startled cries coming from them as he passed.

He tried to keep calm, but his head pounded and his legs screamed. The slap of his rubber soles hitting the stone floor echoed ahead of him. He feared someone would hear him coming, ambush him, but caution wasn't an option. He had to get out of there. He had to!

At one point, he saw a doorway bright with harsh sunlight. Instead of running toward it, he ran away, following the voice's directions. He had to, he needed Bendel to see.

Noah had almost cleared a short flight of stairs when a huge forearm slammed into his chest. The impact sent him tumbling back down the stairs, gasping for air.

His back hurt as he turned over. When he tried to get up, his left hip screamed in protest. His knee gave out on him. He clung to the wall to keep from falling flat on his face. A moment later, a fist clamped onto his throat and hauled him off his feet. He grabbed at it, struggling, unable to even gasp a breath.

Suddenly, in his mind, Bendel whimpered. *No, not now! Please go away!* Noah didn't know who Bendel was talking to, but his vision vanished with that plea. Blind again. Nothing but black.

The alien set Noah back on his feet, but didn't let him go enough to do more than finally take a breath. Then thick fingers and meaty hands twisted Noah's arms behind his back while he cursed and thrashed. He refused to walk, yelling threats he couldn't even begin to carry out. While one alien held his arms, the other lifted him off his feet. Noah kicked out and caught something bony. He heard the alien cry out, hiss, and hoped he'd broken its nose, jaw, *something*.

A fist slammed into his side and another into his—

"I don't...understand."

This was bad. The kind of bad he wouldn't survive.

Another blow to his kidney forced a brief scream out of him.

"Talk weapon," someone said. "Say how."

"*What weapon?*"

Because if he had any goddamn weapons, he'd be using them not talking about them. And, yeah, he knew this was an interrogation complete with torture, but they sucked at the questioning part. Whoever it was that asked the questions barely understood English. He didn't want to think about how they'd gotten the language out of him. He shivered hard, wincing as that jarred his ribs.

And then he smelled it.

"No! Not again. Shit. Fuck. *Fuck.*"

The stinking, tentacled thing latched onto the

uninjured side of his face. Immediately, a pain like he'd never known before seared through his head. His breath froze in his lungs as his body arched involuntarily. Couldn't scream. Couldn't stop it. His brain burned while the rest of him sizzled, twitching.

Finally, the damn thing fell off of him. It plopped onto the ground, and someone swooped in close to grab it up. Noah just gasped and didn't even try to hold back his cries while he slumped against the slimy wall.

Already on his ass after his legs gave out earlier, he twisted away from them all. With his wrists bound over his head, he could hide his face and try to regroup. Not that it would matter. He was pretty damn sure they'd kill him soon.

Still blind—but kinda glad for that now—Noah listened to the brain-burner get eaten. At least, he figured that's what one of his interrogators did with it. Lots of smacking, chomping noises. Whatever that thing was, it helped them learn the language by raping his mind.

Suddenly, the others in here with him had a rapid-fire discussion. A couple of them sounded pissed. This was probably it. Tears leaked down his battered face. He wanted to go out swinging and cursing, but oh, goddamn, he hurt so much. Everything was broken. He didn't want to die, but... He needed all of this to just *end*.

Someone grabbed a fistful of his hair and yanked his head back. He cried out, every muscle tensing. They'd slit his throat. This was it.

"Nothing telling," the alien said. Its breath stank. "More smart later."

And it let him go.

Through the sound of his panicked breathing, Noah heard a lot of slithering around. Heard the door groan. They were leaving?

More smart later... *Fucking-fuck, it's an intermission.*

"Oh, shit," he half-sobbed. He turned back toward the wall.

CHAPTER SIX

FORTRESS DUNGEON

V ivek entered the dungeon during the early morning when the moons were still high in the dark sky. Only three guards were on duty at the entrance between the palace proper and the dungeon. Each would wake in several risings, confused and no doubt hoping their superiors never found out they had fallen asleep. And never suspecting that an Aguadite healer had gently touched them and willed them unconscious.

His hooded black cloak concealed his body from all the tortured eyes that gazed upon him as he passed their cells, but they knew who he was. Many, if not all, had found themselves in his secret care at one time or another during their imprisonment. His instinct to heal would not allow him to let them suffer when he could prevent it. They kept silent as he passed.

He rounded a corner of moldy stone blocks to reach the corridor leading to the larger cells where two or more prisoners were kept in each. Records indicated the Human's was the first one.

Already on his toes to walk, Vivek was able to see through the tiny window in the door. The Human huddled on the floor against the far wall. He stretched the limits of wrist and ankle shackles and was a pale cream color with short black hair on his head and face. His light blue garment was torn and covered with dungeon filth and blood. Vivek's heart ached for him already.

The Human did not react when Vivek opened his noisy door, as he closed it, nor as he walked over to kneel beside him. When he gently touched his arm, though, the male's head snapped up, and Vivek gasped.

One side of his face was purple with bruises and disfigured from swelling. His eye was merely a slit in the bulging flesh. His lips were distorted into a grimace, split, and bleeding. The black film coating his other eye gave clear evidence of the *krikti* they had used on him. The Human's eyes were most likely unharmed as *krikti* was not meant to damage, but the bacteria collected between the cornea and the iris would remain there indefinitely without the antidote or Vivek's intervention. Technically speaking, it was a method of restraint least likely to cause physical harm, but making someone blind left a mark on the psyche that seemed, to him, unforgivable. To then beat that person...

Thoughts of how much trouble this Human would be vanished from Vivek's mind. His blindness and suffering secured him a place under Vivek's protection.

The Human moved jerkily away from Vivek's fingers, mumbling. Vivek did not recognize the language, not having had the chance to learn any Earth ones yet.

Humans were still new enough to the rest of the universe that this was, in fact, Vivek's first encounter with one. In a moment, though, he would copy the Human's knowledge of his language so he could verbally reassure him before he worked to heal him enough to leave.

Vivek unlocked the shackles with the code he had stolen, and they adjusted in size, growing larger. In a moment, each shackle had opened wide enough for the Human's ankle or wrist to slip free.

He gasped with his freedom, but clutched at the slimy wall, hiding his face. *Understandable.* Vivek gently touched the Human's head, petting down his short hair, and murmuring to him in his own native tongue of Sowasish. He knew his patient would not understand, but he listened. As he calmed, he surprised Vivek by turning and reaching toward him with cut and dirty fingers.

Vivek let the Human find his arm and follow it to his face. Despite the fact they were both of the Helokis species, and had similar physical characteristics, Vivek was clearly a being meant for life in and near water. Finding a lack of texture and hair on his skin did not seem to disturb the Human. However, when he touched Vivek's face, discovered his lack of nose and the wide space between his eyes, the Human trembled hard and flinched away.

Needing to reassure him that though he was foreign in appearance he meant no harm, Vivek gently brought one shaking hand back to touch his lips. Surely the Human knew what a smile was.

He did. Tentatively, he smiled back.

Tears suddenly built and spilled from his damaged eyes. "*Pleez*," he whispered hoarsely. He cupped Vivek's cheek, trembling all over now.

Though Vivek did not understand the word, he recognized its meaning all too clearly. He placed his hand over his patient's and nodded his head. When the Human released a tiny sob, tears cascading from his sightless eye, Vivek gathered him into his arms. He could easily offer physical comfort and reassurance. The male came willingly into his embrace and leaned heavily against him. His breath hitched several times and he trembled, his fingers clutching Vivek's robes.

Wanting words now, Vivek cupped the back of his patient's head with one hand. He sent little waves of energy from himself to the Human in the elemental way of his people to ease pain and encourage relaxation. Without the Human feeling more than a pleasant heat, Vivek used his special skills to access his knowledge of his language.

"Fear not," he said, making the Human gasp. "You are safe with me. I will help you."

"You speak English? Who are you?"

"Vivek Korraay," he said quietly. "I am a healer."

"You don't feel like the others looked." His lip re-split and bled.

"I am not like them. I am from Aguada."

"Is that where we are?"

"No, we are on Tev." Through his touch, he asked the Human's body to send him slowly into sleep. They could talk more later. Would have plenty of time to do so, in fact. "Please understand, sir, that I will do my utmost to keep you safe."

"Noah," he said as his blind eye blinked closed. "My name...is Noah."

"These people will not harm you again, Noah." Vivek eased Noah's head into the crook of his elbow, his long, lean body pliant enough to easily lay across his lap without a struggle.

"Thank you...Vivek," he mumbled, before Vivek felt Noah give in to sleep's call.

Vivek let Noah sink down completely into a deep, dreamless sleep. The energy Vivek gave him would keep his body from requiring nutrients, and unconsciousness would allow Vivek an easier time of healing him quickly.

To gain a more direct contact for the healing, Vivek tugged up the filthy shirt until he could see pale skin covered by soft, black hairs. *Interesting.* He really did want to explore, but the healing took priority over curiosity. He pressed his hand against the firm muscle of Noah's upper abdomen and felt the labored rise and fall of his breaths.

As Vivek felt the energy he sought building deep inside him like an inner light, strong and hot, he made a mental note to take more *alinex* as soon as he finished. He recognized and admitted that his curiosity was not merely scientific. The potent drug would diminish the sexual temptation Noah now presented. He should have taken it first, but now simply refused to allow himself to be distracted by the warm musculature and soft hairs under his hand.

The healing energy radiated up from Vivek's core

and down his arm to reach his hand. All other thoughts faded as he focused on Noah's injuries. When his hand began to tingle, he spoke to Noah's battered body, energy to energy.

First, he focused on the most minor of damage. Having never healed a Human before, he felt it necessary to practice on little things like scrapes and bruises. In his mind's eye he watched Noah's body respond appropriately when his skin slowly sealed, changed from angry red to healing pink to unblemished cream in a few counts.

Satisfied a Human's body responded as he hoped, Vivek moved inward, searching Noah's organs and bones for damage. He found more bruises that he willed away. Two fractured ribs knitted back together, firm and strong. Noah's breathing improved after that. One kidney, several groupings of muscles, and a disc in his spine required additional attention. Noah relaxed even more against Vivek's chest once he'd healed those injuries.

Vivek focused harder, digging deep inside himself, and moved to Noah's face. Bones had been shattered, muscles torn, blood vessels broken, but he would heal Noah without a scar or trace of deformity. Vivek poured himself into Noah and felt his body begin to respond to this more intense request to repair itself.

Vivek kept his breathing deep and even as he asked bones, veins, muscles, and skin to realign, grow strong, and return to the way they should be. Every cell complied, as if eager to heal with his help. Noah's cheekbone became strong, the swelling subsided, and two loose teeth fit back into place. His skin seemed to sigh as it relaxed, renewed.

He felt Noah's eyes suffering, then, and asked his energy to destroy the bacteria. It worked, but slowly, and Vivek knew it would require more sessions to accomplish. His energy was draining too rapidly to continue much longer. Once they were safely away, he would have time to try again. For now, Noah should be able to see a blurry image of his surroundings and possibly more clear details up close. It was better than utter darkness, at least.

When Noah's body sent some of Vivek's energies back to him, Vivek shivered and withdrew. The tingling dissipated back down inside him, the glow fading away. He released what felt like a long-held breath and opened his eyes.

Vivek smiled. Noah was lovely. His skin was the pale rosy color of *lilisea* petals and hair as black as the deepest abyss on Aguada was dark, bristly on his jaw, chin, and part of his neck. Noah's features were strong from a sharp nose, lush pink lips, and high cheekbones. He was curiously beautiful.

Vivek held Noah a while longer, savoring the nearness of another living creature. One of such beauty in a harsh and dangerous reality renewed his spirit somewhat. He had plenty of time before one of the guards would awaken, so he simply held Noah while he slept off the effects of the healing.

Eventually, Noah turned, tucking himself against Vivek's chest and looping his arms around his waist. Vivek felt his nether regions reacting with desire. Calmly, because he did not wish to wake Noah and have to explain this, Vivek sifted through a pocket in his robes for the vial of *alinex* to quash his inappropriate attraction.

The alinex dulled his budding arousal and allowed Vivek to explore his patient with a more professional detachment. Normally, that would not have been an issue, but Noah was warm, trusting, and needed him. A heady allure. But with the drug working now, Vivek closed his eyes and let his energy wander within Noah.

Their similarities were truly remarkable.

The same number of bones and configuration of musculature to support them. Vascular and nervous systems were similar, but not exact since Aguadite had additional requirements for aquatic survival. Noah could probably walk on his toes as Vivek had to, but because Noah's feet were clearly built for land movement, he could walk flat-footed while Vivek could not. Did Humans swim well? They appeared built for confinement on land.

Would Noah be able to live beneath the waves on Aguada?

Vivek blinked and stared down at the sleeping Human in his arms. Where had that thought come from?

CHAPTER SEVEN

"How long have I been unconscious?" Noah gingerly moved his head as he lay looking up at the blurry alien.

Vivek's head was bald and he seemed to be wearing a black and blue dress. Robes? Sort of looked like a sorcerer in a fantasy flick. When Vivek came over and crouched down, Noah could see that there was an extra bend to Vivek's legs, like maybe he walked on his bare toes. His long fingers were webbed and his skin had a shiny, rubbery look to its gray-blue color. Reminded Noah of a dolphin he'd swum with once as a kid.

That was it; Vivek was like an anthropomorphic dolphin, but without the long snout. While Noah couldn't quite make out Vivek's features—maybe if he got up in his face he could—Noah could see Vivek had blunt, white teeth when he smiled, no nose, and widely spaced, black eyes.

All together, Vivek seemed really out of place in this snake-filled desert.

"You slept briefly," Vivek said, "but you are well now." He voice was deep and soothing, with just a touch of an accent that sounded almost like a native Italian speaking English.

"My vision's... Well, I couldn't see *any*thing before, so this is better. But is it permanent?" He didn't want to seem ungrateful, but holy fuck if he was stuck half-blind, so helpless... A shiver tracked down his spine.

"We will have to work more on your eyes later, unfortunately. We do not have the time nor do I have the energy to finish that healing process now."

"Oh, sure. That's fine. Okay." A little more of his tension eased away. He could wait patiently for normal sight, knowing it was coming.

Vivek took Noah's hand and helped him up. Only then did Noah realize his wounds were completely *gone*, not just cleaned and bandaged. Touching his face, he discovered that his left eye wasn't even tender. He'd known those bones were broken.

"I was a mess. How did you do this?"

"With a touch, my people can heal most illnesses and injuries."

Healing by touch? Vivek said it so absolutely, like it was no big deal, when Noah would've called it a miracle a minute ago. Shit, back on Earth, everyone would freak to see an alien, but a *magical* alien? They'd chop him up in some government lab just for not being Human, but add on an ability to heal like that and—

Suddenly, Noah had a very vivid moment of clarity regarding his treatment since *Swallowtail* touched down in that landing bay. His people would've done the same and maybe even worse if some alien ship had landed. It made him oddly forgiving as he stared at Vivek staring back at him.

For a minute, anyway.

"I guess I owe you one, then." Noah offered Vivek a smile.

"Noah, it was my honor. There is no debt."

From the way he said it, and the sincerity of his voice, Noah believed him.

"Hey, have you heard from Bendel?"

"Is that something you require?"

"Bendel's a person. He spoke to me in...my mind." Noah cleared his throat. *Oh what the hell.* He was, after all, talking to a magical alien. "I was just wondering if he'd spoken to you, too."

"No, he has not spoken to me. Aguadite are impervious to telepaths who are not also Aguadite. Does Bendel reside within this dungeon as well?"

"Yes." He frowned. "I think so. He was helping me escape, and I was trying to get to him, when they caught me." Absently, he rubbed his hand over his chest.

Vivek sighed as if burdened. "We should leave quickly, but if he could benefit from a healer, I will help him before we depart. Do you have any way of contacting him?"

"He just starts—"

I am here, Bendel's quiet voice said in Noah's mind.

Noah flinched. "He just spoke to me. Said he was here."

Vivek must have smiled because his gray face gained a white curve. "Tell him about me."

"Bendel," he said, feeling strange to be talking to someone who wasn't in the room while someone else watched him do it. "There's a healer named Vivek here with me. We're—"

Please, bring the healer. Please!

A wave of urgency washed through Noah at the sound of Bendel's desperation. "We have to go. He needs you. Bendel, can you do that vision thing you did before? Show me where we need to go to get to you?"

He didn't answer, but Noah could see in that weird way again, like looking through the end of a glass bottle. "Follow me," he said and preceded Vivek to the door.

Vivek grabbed his shoulder, stopping him from leaving. "Follow his directions, but be quiet. I incapacitated some guards, but others may be nearby."

Noah nodded and listened to Bendel as he guided him once again, Vivek following behind him.

This time, Noah didn't run, but it was a similar trip to the previous one. The winding corridors made of pale yellow blocks had plenty of shadows since they were lit only by torches in sconces spaced one every twenty feet or so. The floors were the same rock with a lot of loose grit covering them, so much so several corners had small dunes of the stuff. When they walked by an open doorway that clearly led outside, Noah realized it was night out there.

Finally, they came to a place where the corridor continued straight ahead and also branched in three other directions. Bendel's weird sharing of sight let Noah see partway down all four options. In one of them slithered a snake-monster.

"There's a guard down that way," Noah whispered and pointed. "It's moving away from us, but taking its time about it."

Vivek walked around Noah, his footfalls nearly silent. The guard's shushing movements probably could've hidden it if Vivek ran up behind him. Noah edged closer so he could see farther down the hall just in time for Vivek to reach the guard.

Noah might not have been at the best angle to see everything, but it looked like Vivek barely touched the guard's tail. The thing paused, gave a groan, and then crashed to the ground. A cloud of dust puffed up around it. Vivek watched it all very calmly, before returning to Noah.

"Which way?" Vivek whispered.

Had he killed the guard? With just one touch? Noah was honestly unsure how he felt about Vivek murdering someone, especially when he didn't seem disturbed by what he'd done. It was a good thing he'd done something, of course. The guard had been moving in the direction Bendel needed them to go.

But still, Vivek held the power of life or death in his touch?

Noah took the lead again, but quickly found himself at the edge of a row of cell doors like his own had been. They were thick, dark wood with small, barred windows near the tops, each one spaced very close together. It was like a hallway of really creepy closets with monsters inside them.

Some of them are *monsters*, Bendel said in his mind.

There are very scary creatures in here, Noah. But not all of us are bad.

Since it was possible Noah had felt Bendel's emotions a couple times already, he attempted to send Bendel a mental hug. For some reason, the image that came to mind was of himself standing waist-deep in the perfect waters off the Seychelles. Fine sand, bright sun, clear and warm water lapping at his skin just felt soothing right then so he offered it up.

Beautiful, Noah. I can almost feel it all.

"They will not alert the guards," Vivek said and preceded Noah down the corridor.

Who? Oh, the prisoners. Honestly, Noah hadn't thought of that possibility, but it was good to know. He followed closely behind Vivek in case the inmates' loyalties were to the healer. Then he had to wonder aloud, "Should we release them...or something? Are they like me, I mean?"

"I am certain some are wrongfully imprisoned, yes, while others are criminals. Do you wish to stay and interview them all to determine who is who?"

Noah resisted flicking Vivek off since he'd probably have to explain what it meant. So, fine. There was a part of him that wouldn't appreciate it if some alien disagreed with the penal systems of Earth and just up and freed everyone. There were monsters there, too. It would make a great distraction here and now, though. Plus, leaving these aliens with a mess to clean up sounded like a hell of a good idea.

A tentacle shot out from between the bars of a cell door's window and wrapped around Vivek's upper arm.

Vivek and Noah both hollered in alarm. Noah punched the muscular appendage, and it released Vivek with a series of pops as the red-edged suction cups detached.

"*Noah*. All is well." Vivek caught Noah's wrist before he could hit the thing again.

"What?"

"They merely wished to pay me." Vivek showed Noah a plum-sized yellow stone. "I healed them several turns ago."

The sleek, pale blue tentacle withdrew back into the cell, clicks and snapping sounds chattering at them as something shushed away from the door.

"Oh. Okay." Noah gulped down his shock of adrenaline.

Vivek stuffed the stone into his breast pocket, and then wiped his hand on a section of blue robe over his thigh. He led the way, his long legs eating up the dusty ground. It looked like Vivek had tiny feet... Or maybe he was walking on his toes? Noah bent and squinted, trying to see better. He bumped into Vivek when he suddenly stopped.

"Run!" Vivek hollered before dashing off around a corner.

Noah ran after him. Immediately, he realized Vivek probably meant for him to run the *other* way.

One long guard was already on the ground, but two others kept Vivek back by swinging a club and a spear. Weirdly, Vivek seemed to be parrying with his arms, like he tried to reach past their weapons to strike them with his bare hands. Was he trying to do that touch thing that had taken down the other guard? It was getting more obvious by the second that Vivek wasn't going to win this time.

There was a corridor just behind the guards, perpendicular to the one they stood in. Hoping it was possible to get around behind them, Noah now ran in the opposite direction, looking for a passage to take. After several prisoners' cells, he found a connecting hall and sprinted down it. Luckily, he found himself heading back toward the fight in a few seconds instead of getting lost in a maze of passages.

Cautiously, Noah sidled up to the end of the corridor. Mere feet away, Vivek was still lunging and retreating as the guards did the same. The guards kept hissing, while Vivek remained silent. It was the clearly visibly cuts on Vivek's arms, red blood staining his robes, that urged Noah to act *now*. He couldn't lose Vivek.

Going on the assumption that Vivek would rush in and do the touch thing if an opportunity presented itself, Noah looked for a way to distract the guards. One that wouldn't get him a spear to his gut in the narrow space because, though Bendel's helping sight was great, it was distorted enough that Noah's perception could be way off when he needed accuracy.

The torch. In a metal wall sconce secured to the stone wall was a length of wood crowned by a cup. The glossy contents fed the flames that lit this section of the corridor. Noah grabbed the torch, hefted it, and bashed the nearest guard in the center of his back.

The howl out of him made Noah flinch since the fire's fuel now coated the snake-alien's head and shoulders. Noah backed off quickly, and Vivek dove in to touch both guards. They collapsed almost immediately.

Noah stood there watching the flames continue to flicker over the snake-monster's long, thick, black body. He couldn't smell anything.

"He will not burn," Vivek said in between panted breaths. "The fire only consumes its fuel. His flesh will heat, but should not become damaged."

Nodding, Noah didn't correct Vivek. "What now?" he asked, scanning the corridor.

Suddenly, Noah's heart sped up all over again with a panic he didn't understand. His Bendel-given vision faded back to his own blurry version.

I cannot maintain the connection through the pain this machine causes me, Bendel said in Noah's mind. *I will... I will reconnect. I apologize, Noah.*

"It's okay, baby. It's okay." There was such an ache in Noah's chest from knowing something hurt Bendel but he couldn't stop it. Why did he care so much?

Was Bendel *making* him care?

CHAPTER EIGHT

"What is wrong?" Vivek walked back toward Noah. He seemed amazingly uninjured now that Noah could see him up close.

"I've lost the connection with Bendel. Something—a machine—is hurting him." He couldn't help rubbing at his chest where his heart still beat a little too fast.

"He is not among these cells as I have been here many times. Also, a machine would require electricity and there is none in this wing. I believe the newer section is this way." He indicated the direction he had been going.

"Okay, let's go." Noah squinted, trying to make out shapes from the light and shadow.

"Unless..."

Noah stopped. "Unless what?"

"Unless you would prefer to leave now that he is no longer connected to you."

Vivek said it kindly, he did, but just the idea of abandoning Bendel made Noah feel sick. "I can't. There's more of a connection between us than the telepathy. It's like we're emotionally linked, too. I might be feeling what he feels."

"You think he is controlling you?"

"I don't know." The possibility made him shudder.

"I have no way of verifying if your health could be affected by his." Vivek squeezed Noah's shoulder for a moment. "If you are connected, then we must retrieve him as well to ensure your health." Vivek started walking again, and Noah followed. "I have not been into the newer section of the dungeon because I was concerned about surveillance. You concentrate on listening for guards, and I will focus on avoiding cameras."

"Aren't you here to heal the inmates? I thought you were the doctor or something."

Without turning, Vivek said, "I heal them because I cannot allow them to suffer when I have the ability to stop it."

Noah was fully aware Vivek had chosen not to confirm or deny whether healing was his reason for being here. While he followed Vivek as quietly as he could down another corridor, Noah decided to let the matter drop. Now wasn't the time for probing discussions.

Though, he did wish he knew who else didn't deserve to be trapped here.

You cannot save everyone.

"Bendel!" Noah bit his lips together after that holler.

I heard you! You are close to me.

Vivek halted and asked, "Has he reconnect—"

"He said he heard me say his name." Noah had to

consciously make himself stop flapping his arms like a damn bird. "Uh... We've got to be close."

Thankfully, Vivek seemed excited, too. "Ask him to make a noise."

"Make some kind of noise for us, baby." *Baby? What are you doing calling him baby?*

A weak little giggle reverberated in his head. *I do not mind the endearment so much right now. I need help. Please help me*, he said the last with clear desperation.

"There," Vivek said. "Is he doing that?"

"Are you making that noise? Thud-thud-thud?" he said in time to the nearby pounding.

Yes. My foot on the table.

"That's him."

"Come on." Vivek moved stealthily down the hall toward Bendel's slow beat. It started to have longer moments of silence in between thumps.

"Keep kicking the table, Bendel. We're close."

So tired. Please hurry.

"We have to hurry," he whispered to Vivek. "Making that noise is wearing him out."

Vivek paused where the corridor dead-ended with a doorway and two branching halls leading left or right. "I believe he is in there." Vivek pointed ahead of them.

"Make one big noise, honey. I think we're almost there."

The sound he heard then was a cross between a sob and a scream. It definitely came from the room ahead of them. Noah held his breath to stop himself from crying out, too.

Vivek checked both ways, then ushered Noah into the room ahead of him.

No door, no guards. Why bother? Bendel was a child strapped down to a wooden table with thin, stiff tubes of dark red poking out of his spindly, little body from arms, chest, abdomen and thighs. The machine those tubes went into was a sleek, modern piece of equipment totally out of place in this primitive dungeon.

Even with Noah's bad eyesight, he could see that this was a really scared kid undergoing a horrific medical experiment. Noah could clearly hear Bendel's rattling, gasping breaths and small whimpers, like the poor kid was slowly dying. It definitely did not look like anything in that room was there to help him live.

They take my blood to test it.

"Why?" Noah whispered, his voice hoarse.

They want my abilities.

Noah didn't know what that meant as he stood by Bendel's side, unable to touch him or tear his eyes from him. On the other side of the table, Vivek reached out slowly and placed his hand on Bendel's forehead. Noah felt like dropping to his knees and praying, or maybe running from the room. He just stood there.

He had been right to call him baby; the kid barely looked more than eight years old.

Suddenly, Bendel's weak body began to expel the needles and their tubes as if his skin spat them out. Vivek placed his other hand in the center of Bendel's chest. The boy gasped. The wounds all over him closed to form little scabs. After a moment, those faded away. His coloring improved and his sweat seemed to evaporate.

Just like *that*.

When Vivek removed his hands, he stumbled like his knees gave out. He braced his hands on the table.

Noah went to help him. "Vivek?"

"That was more than I meant to do."

Considering what he'd said about using his own energy to heal others, they were probably lucky Vivek hadn't passed out. Neither he nor Bendel could make it out of here on their own.

"What do you need? Are you okay?"

"I am well."

"You're not. Don't lie to me, man. Just tell me what you need."

Vivek gave him a small, patient smile. "Nothing here will help me, Noah." He patted Noah's arm. "Leaving is the best thing we can do."

Vivek lifted the boy and made to give him to Noah. He shook his head, but then realized it made sense for him to carry Bendel. He didn't know the way out of the dungeon. He couldn't lead them without Bendel's aid. He couldn't protect them. He was useless as anything other than a pack mule.

"Wait," he said as inspiration struck. He undid his flight suit to take off his undershirt, and then helped Bendel into it, giving him at least that much to cover up the kid's nakedness. Carefully, Noah accepted the boy into his arms.

Bendel rested his head on Noah's shoulder, his forehead pressed to his neck, and his little body cradled close to his chest. His arms were limp in his lap as he sighed. He weighed less than nothing and said not a word out loud or telepathically, but Noah thought he might've felt Bendel smile.

Whispering, Noah asked, "Why would they hurt him like this?"

Vivek cleared his throat. "I do not know." He steered them out of the room ahead of him. "Wait here. I cannot leave anything behind."

Before Noah could ask how Vivek intended to carry that machine, he heard a strange *whoosh* sound. He spun around. The whole room burned, and Vivek stood beside the table like the fire couldn't touch him. And maybe it couldn't.

Vivek picked up a dark jar. Was it filled with Bendel's blood? Vivek stared at it, and Noah wished he could see his expression. But then he didn't need to as, with a wordless yell, Vivek pitched the jar at the far wall. It shattered, contents spraying, and the flames leapt higher.

Vivek brushed by Noah and kept walking. "Follow me, Noah. We leave this place *now*."

Noah rushed after Vivek.

CHAPTER NINE

F inally outside the palace, Vivek took deep breaths of the cool, fresh night air, grateful this part of their escape was over. Through all his time on Ulvar, he had been unable to resist the call to heal those trapped within the dungeon. The despair had chafed at the essence of him. He could not have saved every individual, but it felt good now to leave the dungeon behind with Noah and Bendel. Vivek offered up a hope that with the downfall of the alliance, King Solong's rule might end and the dungeon be emptied out after his fall.

With Bendel cradled in his arms, Noah came up alongside Vivek. "Are you killing the guards when you touch them?"

"*No*. I would never *kill*," Vivek said, aghast. "I force them to sleep."

"Oh. Okay."

Vivek could not interpret the look on Noah's face. Continued concern? For himself?

"Noah, my people have the ability to manipulate the

energies within others and ourselves. While our history may include foul acts committed by those who believed themselves above reproach, for several generations we have adhered to a philosophy of nonviolence and compassion."

Noah stepped closer, his clouded eyes taking in every nuance of Vivek's expression. Vivek let him look, hoped he saw the truth.

"We went so far as to fully declare our abilities to the Coalition of Planets when we requested to join.Were I not on this mission and concealing my true self, I would openly proclaim the level of my skills by wearing a band here." Vivek pointed at his upper left arm. "We do not hide who we are nor what we can do."

Nodding, Noah smiled. "Thanks. It was...worrying me, I guess." He glanced down at Bendel. "Knowing he might be manipulating me and wondering if you were, too."

Vivek gripped Noah's shoulder. "What I have done up to this point was for your benefit alone. From now onward, I will only do what you allow."

Noah nodded again and resumed walking. Vivek kept quiet, giving the Human time to process all that he had been through.

Soon enough, they entered the winding streets of the surrounding village. On both sides were one- and two-story yellow stone buildings packed close together. A few establishments had fires lit and a few curious eyes silently watched them pass. Given that others not native to Tev moved about the streets at this early hour, Vivek hoped his small group would prove unremarkable.

Noah's sudden question startled Vivek. "Where are we going?"

"My...residence."

"Then what do we do?"

Vivek sighed and slowed down until Noah came abreast of him. "We will take what supplies we can to where I've hidden my ship and then leave this planet."

"Leave the whole planet? Wow. Okay. Where will we go?"

Noah's murky eyes flicked all over Vivek's face as if desperate to see something clearly. Noah must be a male accustomed to being in charge. Vivek took pity on him. He rested a hand on Noah's shoulder and encouraged him to walk beside him.

"I need to enter Coalition space," Vivek said, "to relay information to my superiors. To do so from here could result in any number of complications, and I need this information to arrive whole, encrypted, and to the party I intend."

"What's the information?"

Vivek shook his head. "I would prefer not to say in the open like this."

Honestly, it would not matter if he told Noah what he knew since he doubted the Tevian living around them knew Earth's English language. But this was the most sensitive of details and he did not wish to risk it should anything happen to them. They were not far enough away yet to be considered successfully out of Solong's reach.

"Are you some kind of spy?"

"It would be best if we were quiet through here."

Noah looked around, alternating between squinting and widening his eyes. He adjusted his hold on Bendel. When he paused to look around some more, Vivek grasped Noah's upper arm and tugged him along.

They left the residential area and passed through the barren crop fields. Two full moons overhead provided plenty of light to see by as they finally reached the cliff. He had Noah wait as he dropped down onto the first of three small ledges jutting out over the river far below.

"Crouch down, then pass Bendel to me."

"Right," Noah said, sounding breathless. He moved slowly, his eyes wide. Vivek regretted not being able to clear Noah's eyes more so he would be less fearful now. "Jesus." He leaned forward so Vivek could take Bendel from him.

Vivek settled Bendel on his hip, one arm supporting his little bottom. Bendel's small hands fisted Vivek's robes.

"Jesus?" Vivek asked with honest curiosity, but also as a possible distraction for Noah. Given the male's penchant for chatter, encouraging that might help him calm his fears.

"Religious figure."

"Ah. Sit down on the edge, so I can reach you and help you down."

Noah sat, and then scooted forward. He did not appear at all confident that this would be successful.

Vivek reached up and gripped Noah's forearm. "I promise you, Noah, I will not let you fall."

"Sure."

"I am stronger than you."

"Vivek, we're the same size *and* you're holding Bendel."

He could hold twenty children and still be able to pick Noah up. "Please trust me a little while longer."

Noah took a deep breath and nodded, his hand gripping Vivek's upper arm as well. Using that connection, Vivek pulled Noah down onto the ledge. He ignored Noah's yelp.

"I will send you down to the next ledge first this time." He had to pull Noah to get him near the edge again.

"Wait. I think—" Noah gasped, his other arm flailing as Vivek forced him over the edge and dangled him down to the next ledge. "Son of a bitch!"

Vivek frowned since neither definition of that last word was complimentary to his mother. "I hope that is not in reference to my parentage."

"Sort of. Christ, tell me we're close to being wherever the hell we're going."

"Christ?" Vivek hopped down to stand again in front of Noah.

"Same religious figure. Jesus Christ." Noah took a deep breath, his face pale and eyes wide. "Come on, man, answer the question."

"There was no question, Noah." Vivek quickly dropped him down to the last ledge.

"Fuck!" Noah's voice echoed across the canyon. "All right, if you're trying to prove you're stronger, I fucking believe you. Let me go." He tried to shake his arm free once Vivek joined him.

Smiling down at Bendel smiling up at him, Vivek let

Noah go, though he did stand between him and the edge. Panting, Noah clung to the cliff face behind him.

Vivek forced his smile away and tried to sound sincere. "I apologize, Noah. I felt a quick, forced descent might prove easiest."

"Yeah, whatever." He pointed at Bendel. "No, I don't need to change my pants, pipsqueak."

Vivek glanced at Noah's groin, and then away. There were no stains, but there was an intriguing bulge. Did a Human's genitalia remain outside their bodies at all times? How unsafe.

Vivek turned toward the mouth of the cave. He grasped the pyro-stick he had left there after his last visit. He knocked the stick against his thigh. Immediately, it flashed to life, and Noah flinch, covering his eyes. Vivek winced.

"I apologize." Vivek turned his back on Noah and kept the light in front of him. "Your eyes will be sensitive to light until I can heal them more. Just follow behind me now."

Vivek made sure Noah had a hold of his shoulder before walking them into the tunnel that gently sloped deeper into the ground.

"You live underground? You look made to be underwater."

"My people do live beneath the surface of the ocean on Aguada. This place is only temporary until my mission is complete." He allowed himself to smile. "Which it now is."

"Mission?"

He could not use the rouse of needing to be silent

now, so admitted it. "You were correct, Noah. I am a spy. I plan to prevent an alliance that could plunge the universe into war."

Noah made a whistling sound. "This place just keeps getting weirder and weirder. I feel like I've fallen down that fucking rabbit hole."

Relying on his new language definitions, Vivek said, "I do not think fuck means what you think it does, Noah."

"Ha! I know what it means, Vivek. Don't worry about that." He suddenly laughed again, this time with more humor, and reached to tap Bendel's head. "You're too young for thoughts like that, kiddo."

Bendel just hummed faintly. Vivek was tempted to push the boy into sleep, but he had already used quite a bit of his own energy reserves and there was still much to do. Only when he had his ship on autopilot toward Coalition space could he indulge in the rest he needed to revitalize himself.

What would he do with Noah and Bendel after he was able to send his message and return to Aguada? Free of his duties and finally able to return to a normal life—whatever that was anymore—there would be no place for an adult Human and a child of unknown origin. What could he possibly do with them?

CHAPTER TEN

Despite the bright white light stick Vivek held, the darkness surrounding Noah inside the sloped tunnel made him feel boxed in. After having nearly pissed himself during that "dangling Noah" stunt, his heart pounded in his chest and he couldn't quite catch his breath. A sudden case of claustrophobia did not help him calm down. But he knew what to do. He breathed in through his nose and out through his mouth and stared at the ceiling above Vivek's head.

The tunnel walls were rough where they'd cracked, but overall it was the kind of smooth he thought might be from water erosion. The rock was dark brown with veins of a clear crystal that glittered all around them in the light of Vivek's stick. *All right, that's kind of pretty.* Noah felt himself finally calming. He'd probably be tense for the rest of his life, but this wasn't bad right now.

Just as the air took on a damp basement quality, the tunnel opened up to a larger, water-ravaged cave. Vivek stabbed the light stick into the ground near him, and then walked deeper into the space. Shielding his eyes, Noah stayed where he was for a moment, trying to focus on the ground. When he could see the pocked stone a bit better, he moved around until the light was behind him.

A few feet in front of Noah, the gray and blue shape that was Vivek set down the tan and white bundle that was Bendel. Maybe on a pile of blankets? He could hear Bendel sigh from here. Vivek opened something shiny on top of an orange crate. Not knowing what else to do with himself—and definitely not asking for direction—Noah looked around some more.

The whole space wasn't that big since Noah could see enough definition to pick out the glittering, curved walls. The cave ceiling might've had stalagmites, but Noah's depth perception was off. He could see the light reflecting off puddles all around him, though. The whole place was moist, chilly, and depressing.

How had Vivek lived here?

Something dark caught Noah's eye just before a foot-long millipede bug thing suddenly wove around his foot.

He gasped and clapped a hand over his mouth as he lifted his foot. The creature continued on its way, weaving around puddles and rocks. Sweet fuck, he was so done with things that slithered. Only once the little bastard had disappeared into a crack along the wall of the cave did Noah tore his eyes away and looked to Vivek.

Hello! Noah's vision was pretty blurry at this distance, but it was clear enough to let him see Vivek getting naked over there. Noah crossed his arms like he waited somewhat impatiently, sighed a few times like he was bored, and looked at Vivek through the fringe of his eyelashes.

Was Vivek male? Noah had labeled him male right away, but nothing about the blurry, gray shapes of him helped identify him one way or another. Maybe his kind didn't have distinct genders? Noah rubbed at his eyes, as if that would help him get a better look.

"Noah, I need you to change as well." Vivek slid black pants up his legs.

Noah looked down at himself. His flight suit was dirty, possibly a little blood-stained, but so what? "Why?"

"Your clothing is too conspicuous. The design is odd for the typical dress of most who might trade on or travel via this planet." He pulled something else black from the crate and put it on like a jacket. Actually, a vest since Vivek's gray arms were still bare. "Even the closure is unique to my knowledge."

"You don't have zippers?" He carefully made his way to Vivek's side. The ground was pocked with little puddles, and Noah's booties weren't meant for outside his ship.

At least now that Vivek was dressed, Noah couldn't be accused of ogling him. Would Vivek even mind that? How did Vivek's people view same-sex, inter-species relationships?

Was he actually thinking about sex while trying to escape an alien planet? *Really, dipshit?*

"We have stickseal," Vivek said, "and auto-sizing. Both are far more practical."

Noah unzipped his flight suit, revealing the plain blue cotton shorts he had on underneath. He hesitated to take his foot out of the suit since all he had on were socks. The bootie attached to his flight suit had a thin rubber sole, but at least it was something.

"Do you have an extra pair of shoes?" Noah asked. "Because we'll have to cut the feet off my suit here if you don't." He would *not* walk around barefoot in this cave of creepy-crawlies. His skin broke out in gooseflesh.

"I do not wear shoes, per se." He gestured toward his feet.

"Oh, hey. Are you standing flat-footed now?" Because Vivek's feet were somewhere near twenty-four inches like this. And he was a lot shorter.

"I am." He shifted his weight back and forth. "I do not walk well. We...we evolved in ways that allow us to function on land, but our main—"

"It's okay, Vivek. I think you're amazing." He touched his smooth forearm. "I just hadn't noticed before and I sometimes blurt things out."

Vivek closed his eyes for a moment. "I have been away from Aguada for some time and am often judged for being unique among a local population."

"I wasn't judging you. I promise."

Vivek nodded. "Perhaps you think I am as interesting as I find you?"

"Exactly." Noah smiled. "So I hope you won't mind me asking questions. Give me the benefit of the doubt that I'm not being mean if I say something stupid."

"Agreed. If you will show me the same courtesy."

"Deal."

Vivek closed the lid on the crate. "Remove what you

can of your clothing, and then sit here. I will separate the feet so you may continue to wear that part."

Noah hopped up onto the crate, and Vivek peeled the rest of the suit off Noah's legs and feet. Vivek held the flight suit up, turning it around, and clearly examining it. Noah just watched him while he sat there in his boxer briefs and socks. Back up on his toes, Vivek moved around behind Noah to lay out his flight suit and slice off the feet just above the ankle with what looked like a black dagger.

Noah turned back around. His great-grandfather's dagger was just another piece of rubble inside the remains of the *Swallowtail*. He shivered and wrapped his arms around himself. He didn't want to think about what he'd planned to do with that knife just before everything had changed. Didn't want to wonder which would've been better.

Vivek came back around in front of Noah and helped him get the booties back on. They looked ridiculous, but they'd do. Hopefully there were aliens out there somewhere who wore shoes and might trade him for a pair. If he ever had something to trade.

"Hop down," Vivek said. "What I need you to wear is still inside the crate."

Noah got down, and Vivek put his flight suit inside the crate. Noah felt ridiculous in his underwear and makeshift shoes. And then Vivek presented him with a long, black dress.

"You're kidding me."

"No, it is not a joke."

"I'm not wearing a dress."

Vivek held it up to Noah's chest like he was checking the length against Noah's height. "This is what a religious cleric might wear, but only when combined with the white overcoat. We will forego that, and you should appear more as a— As a peasant."

Noah pointed at him. "That's not what you were going to say."

Vivek sighed and gathered up the dress in his hands. Before he answered, he popped Noah's head through the neck of the dress and gave it a tug so it fluttered oh so prettily to his knees. Then he said, "A slave."

"Oh, fuck you." Noah hiked the dress up to take it back over his head, but Vivek kept blocking him. "I am *not* posing as your *slave*, you bastard. Let me go!"

"No one would believe a Human cleric, Noah." Vivek grabbed both of Noah's wrists in a hard grip, showing off that super-strength again. "You cannot wear your garment, and this is all I have left."

Noah didn't relax his arms, but did stop trying to wriggle free. "What about the clothes you took off?"

"Healer's robes."

"So another profession a lowly Human can't fake."

Vivek released Noah's wrists. "Your race is not inferior, but yes, you cannot fake either profession." He exhaled harshly. "I do apologize, Noah. Wearing this, posing as a slave, will *not* make you belong to me. I would never attempt to own you." He grinned, flashing white teeth in a pink mouth. "It would take far too much effort to make you submit."

Noah glared but thrust his arms through the sleeve holes that bared his shoulders and arms. He wouldn't think of it as something a slave wore, but as the dress it looked like. Just a dumb dress. He also didn't—and then in not doing it, did it—think about the fact he liked a little submission with his sex.

So not the time, slave boy.

Apparently finished dressing, humiliating, and causing inappropriate thoughts, Vivek said, "We cannot take these the crates with us. They were left by an advance team, and my ship is too far from here for us to haul them. Do you wish to take your clothing?"

Noah set his hand on his flight suit. Logically, practically, it didn't make sense to take it with him. He understood that he needed to blend in, so he'd probably never wear it again. Right now, it was just a souvenir from a life that wasn't his anymore.

"What about just this piece?" Vivek said and traced around the Aviary Corporation patch for the moon colony transport ships.

Noah picked up his flight suit and attempted to rip the patch off. Vivek produced the black knife again. "Can you see well enough?" Vivek asked as he held the grip toward Noah.

"Yes," he said, not even having to lie, and took the blade.

Carefully, he cut the patch free, then did the same with the American flag patch as well. One represented the achievement of his dreams for a space flight career. The other, well, it was just home.

Vivek held out his hand. "I can carry them in a utility pocket of my pants."

"Thank you," Noah said and handed them over.

Vivek put them away before he walked toward Bendel. "Noah, would you like a blanket?"

"We're not staying here for a while, are we?"

If they were, he wanted a blanket to hide under so the fucking alien bugs couldn't get up his dress. Slither along his bare thighs. Lay eggs in his nut sack. Noah scratched at himself as he followed Vivek to Bendel's nest.

"No, we are leaving," Vivek said. "However, we can only take with us what we can carry, so if you would like a blanket, take one now and keep it with you at all times."

Noah figured it might be a good idea to have a blanket since he didn't have anything to carry things in. Well, if he ever got *things*. Maybe where they were headed would be colder than this desert.

And Vivek hadn't said Noah couldn't have a shawl to go with his dress.

Noah decided to wrap Bendel in another blanket. It would help keep him covered up, which would be a good thing. The poor kid had been through enough without flashing his little bits all over the planet. Thankfully, the dove gray blankets were really soft, like a thick fleece.

Bendel's eyelids fluttered, but he didn't open them as he sighed. Noah ended up sort of swaddling the kid in two blankets, making it easier to carry them and Bendel. Noah hoped the kid wouldn't get too hot. Bendel actually looked pretty cute when Noah was done turning him into a big burrito.

Noah lifted Bendel up, assuming they were ready to leave now, and found Vivek standing close enough to him that Noah could see his small smile. The alien healer-spy seemed as charmed by Bendel as Noah was.

"Time to go?"

"Yes. Let us hurry."

When they reached the clear area before the tunnel, instead of taking the light stick, Vivek broke it. The thing shattered into dust, but the cave didn't darken completely. Noah was able to see the faint illumination of a possible dawn shining down at them. If he could see that much with his bad eyes, Vivek could probably see more.

And then there was Vivek's glowing—which Noah didn't mention this time.

"Can you see, Noah?"

"Enough, yeah."

"Come then."

Vivek had Noah lead while carrying Bendel. Going out felt much better than going in had, except for wondering what torture Vivek had planned for getting him back up those damn outcroppings. Swinging him? Throwing him? Noah swallowed hard and reminded himself that he trusted Vivek.

When they stood out in the open again, Noah looked toward the sun rising right along the path of the canyon. The colors were just a bit off, maybe a little more pale than a sunrise back home in Utah. What really had his attention was the way the canyon walls sparkled. Like how Vivek's light stick had made the veins of crystal glitter in the tunnel, the rising sun made the canyon wink and flash.

"Noah."

"Yeah?" He turned and realized Vivek was already above him on the next ledge.

Vivek reached down. "Can you hold Bendel with one arm?"

"Test me."

Noah held Bendel close and gave Vivek his hand. Vivek had them clasp forearms, then lifted Noah up just enough for his feet to clear the rock.

"Go," Noah said, then hung there, stunned, as Vivek simply stood up. Noah got his feet on the ledge, and Vivek steadied him.

And then Vivek did all that twice more. He really was amazingly strong.

When they stood back on the ground and not another rocky outcropping, Noah felt a tremor beneath his feet and heard a muffled explosion.

"What the hell was that?"

Vivek dusted off his hands and adjusted his vest. "I could not risk someone discovering my location and supplies. The explosion was deep enough underground it should not disturb anyone in town."

He'd set off a *bomb*? Noah rubbed at his face and adjusted Bendel. At least Vivek had timed it right.

"That giant bug is either toast or really pissed right now."

He hadn't meant to say that out loud. He could see Vivek squinting at him, probably having trouble with all that slang. Noah looked down at Bendel to see if he understood, but the kid was still passed out.

"Is he going to be okay?"

"Rest is good for him right now. Do you need me to carry him?"

"No, I can handle it."

It was the one thing he could do competently on his own at the moment, so he'd do it. He needed Vivek to be able to defend them, negotiate, or whatever else might be required to get them on their way. So he'd be a pack mule for a sick and exhausted kid if that was the only help he could offer right now. That was how they were going to make it.

CHAPTER ELEVEN

ALIEN DESERT

"Vivek?"

"No, we are not there yet."

Noah cleared his throat. Apparently, he'd asked *that* question a few too many times. Really, though, it seemed like they were walking into the middle of a desert, so it wasn't a dumb question.

"Actually, I'm curious about all the types of...people I've seen so far."

Vivek stopped on top of a low dune and waited for Noah to catch up. "May I carry him for a while?"

"Sure. Thanks."

Noah handed Bendel over to give his arms a rest. The kid wasn't that heavy, but he was a little awkward to carry while walking on sand. Vivek moved on, but slower this time.

"I am uncertain where to begin," he finally said with a glance at Noah.

Noah nodded. There was probably a lot he needed to know just for basic survival purposes. Starting small might help. "How about with you and me? Are we different species?"

"No, we are the same species. It is called Helokis. Simply put, a species is defined by genetic compatibility. The Tevian, for example, are a different species from ours."

He was genetically compatible with Vivek? What in hell would their kid look like? *A pink land-dolphin.* Noah cleared his throat so he wouldn't laugh. *Good lord.* It was ludicrous and kind of wow at the same time.

"Um, what's Tevian?"

"The Ulvar guards."

"You said Tevian. What's Ulvar?"

Vivek huffed a laugh. "This planet is called Tev, which also lends its name to the species of the inhabitants, the Tevian. The country we are in now rules the rest of the planet and is called Ulvar."

"Oh. Okay. Well, anyway no breeding with any of the Tevian species. I'm so disappointed there." He rolled his eyes. *As if...*

Vivek's voice pitched high as he said, "You were *attracted?*" He cleared his throat. "Forgive me, I did not realize. Are you able to carry offspring? Did you—"

"Whoa! Hold on. I was joking. They're snake-monsters, for shit's sake." He exaggerated a shudder.

"Ah, I see." Vivek gave a throaty chuckle. "I try not to judge, but I agree with your assessment."

Not wanting to think about those things ever again, Noah said, "Why'd you ask if I can carry offspring? I'm male."

"Some males of our species can. I only know of

Human physiology what I encountered while healing you. As your genital area was uninjured, I did no further investigation there."

"Oh. Huh. Well, Human males don't give birth." But other races in their species could? *Wow.* "Can you?"

"With the proper...surgical modifications, yes. And those would be passed down to my male children. Other races are biologically predisposed to bear young."

Noah wasn't going to ask, but took that to mean Vivek was male if the modifications would be passed down to his male children. How that thrilled him wasn't appropriate or all that sane. But there it was: he was kind of attracted to Vivek.

"So, um, you adjust your genetics surgically, but you can heal with a touch?"

Vivek frowned thoughtfully. "The word I want to use is not among your English ones." He waved that away. "There is a transfer of energies, a sort of duplication and addition, that would allow me to take on the necessary characteristics to support and deliver offspring. There would be no cutting or healing as your surgery word implies. It is a mostly painless and quick procedure."

"That is absolutely fascinating."

To have some energy transfer accomplish gender reassignment or organ transplants without scarring, healing, possible complications, or even the risk of death? It would be a dream-come-true and a complete miracle for some, yet Vivek said it like it was no big deal.

"Have you?" Noah asked.

"Have I?"

"Been modified to have babies?"

"No. Should my eventual partner and I agree, either he or I may choose to modify to bear our children." Vivek shrugged, and then held Bendel in the crook of one arm. "Perhaps we would both modify to share the experience."

And as fascinating as all that was, there was only one word Noah clung to. "He?"

"I have ever been attracted to my own gender." Vivek looked at Noah. "Is same-gender attraction not possible for humans?"

"Uh, yes, it's possible. There are a lot of different sexualities."

"What is yours?"

"I'm E-zero. Total same-gender attraction, I mean."

Vivek smiled. "I should very much like to discuss Human psychology and physiology with you. Perhaps once we are safe in Coalition space?"

Oh yay. He was a science experiment. "Sure."

"Excellent. I have always enjoyed learning about the various races."

It was stupid how much of Noah's enthusiasm for the discussion died after realizing Vivek wasn't even remotely interested in him specifically. Stupid because it shouldn't matter. Shouldn't even be on his mind! *Alien planet, dumb ass. Aliens who were happy to beat the shit out of you. Aliens who torture little kids.* This was not the time, the place, or even the guy.

Noah let the conversation lag and concentrated on what little he could see around him. Unfortunately, it wasn't much. What visual clarity he had stopped about two feet from his nose. Either a vague hill or flat plain ahead of them were all he could really make out. Letting

Vivek walk in front of him gave him something to focus on besides his own sweatiness and the too-dry wind ruffling his dress around his shins.

Abruptly, Vivek stopped.

"Something wrong?" Noah asked. Vivek's posture said yes, but Noah couldn't see anything more than another hill in front of them. "What is it?"

Vivek didn't answer, but he did shove Bendel into Noah's arms before he ran toward the hill.

Noah opened his mouth to yell at him, but thought better of it. If Vivek ran toward danger, some enemy, it wouldn't help to distract him or call attention to himself. And there was no way Vivek was running *away* from danger. Noah might not have known him long, but he was sure Vivek wasn't the type to cut and run.

So Noah listened, but only heard the whistling wind and Vivek's voice. The snarl in the words had to mean he was cursing. When the rising sun reflected off of something metallic, Noah started walking again. Had they made it to Vivek's—

"Someone ransacked my ship!"

"*Shit.*"

As Noah walked closer, he caught a whiff of decaying vegetation. Was the hill ahead of him actually an oasis? When the ground beneath his feet squished, he figured he was right. Now he could make out towering trees with a boxy shape and large, teardrop leaves. Tucked into and partially covered by shorter plants, apparently, Vivek's ransacked ship. Noah couldn't tell it apart from anything else.

"Did they just take supplies?"

"Components, too. Wiring, half the control panel is gone, and the door as well." More cursing followed that horrible news, then a *thunk* like Vivek kicked the ship.

"So it's not—"

"It is *useless*, Noah. I should never have left it here, but there were so few options and the sun was rising... We cannot fly out on this pile of rotting excrement now." Another kick.

"Shit."

"What?"

"Another word for excrement."

"Shit. Yes." Another kick. "Rotting *shit*."

Noah let him have a moment, figuring every kick to the ship was actually meant for Vivek's own ass. Maybe he'd made a dumb mistake or maybe he hadn't, Noah wasn't in a position to call him on it.

Vivek took a deep breath and sighed it out slowly. Finally, he said, "We will have to find alternative transportation." Even pissed off and he was still so proper.

"Can we steal a ship?"

"I know only how to fly this one model and the likelihood of finding another one—"

"We might as well look for the parts to fix this one?"

"That is not an option."

He hadn't really meant it as one, but fine, good to know.

Vivek came back to him and crossed his arms, head bowed. "We will have to book passage with a transport."

"Can we? I mean, do you have the money for it? Clearance or...something?"

Vivek waved that off. "I have plenty of credits at my disposal, and travel to and from Tev is not restricted."

Suddenly, the sun crested the hill behind Noah and sparked off the metal of Vivek's ship.

"It is the time delay that worries me most," Vivek said, gazing toward the sunrise. "The information I have must be delivered within eight turns. Sooner would be better, given the Coalition must have forces able to intervene by then."

Noah felt stupid having to ask but... "Um. What's a turn?"

"A day, just a more universal term for it since not every planet turns at the same rate of speed."

"Okay. So, where do we go to book passage on a ship off this rock?"

"Right. Yes." Vivek gave another almighty sigh. "We will have to go through a warehouse district and the market to reach the transportation hub." He moved closer to Noah, laying a hand on his shoulder. "Noah, going through these places will require us to play our parts where, before, it was merely a precaution should someone discover us during our journey here."

"Our parts? Oh. The master and slave thing."

"I do apologize, but it is for your safety. Bendel's as well. It is the only explanation that would truly place you under my care and prevent anyone from laying claim to either of you." Vivek's hand slid down to Noah's biceps in a slow caress.

"I understand." Noah stood up a little straighter. "I'll do what I have to to get away."

He'd think of it as going undercover. Given that the

guy with him basically *was* undercover and all super alien spy anyway, it wasn't that far from the truth. He could play along.

"Thank you, Noah."

Noah believed Vivek was no more happy about the dynamic than he was. Would Bendel care? Depending on how long he slept, he might never know.

"Lead the way, then, oh great and powerful master mine." Noah bowed and made a sweeping gesture before nearly dropping Bendel.

Vivek laughed. "Yes, do come along, my sarcastic but most-valued slave."

Noah smiled and followed Vivek again, stupidly pleased.

CHAPTER TWELVE

Vivek silently railed at himself during the walk from his destroyed ship back to the market district near the palace. It was a mystery to him how someone had found his ship or why they might have even been out there with the ability to strip it and haul the parts away. Could someone have followed him when he checked it last? He sighed and tried to push the frustration away as they crested the hill overlooking the market tents.

The sun was getting hot on their backs now. In the valley below, the market bustled as vendors set up their stalls. Vivek could already smell the nauseating scent of roasting meats as smoke from the fire pits drifted upwards. They would need supplies, for even on a passenger ship food was not always included. Enough for at least two turns should be plenty. In that amount of time, they could get quite far and change ships if necessary.

"Carefully here," he said and took Bendel from Noah again so he could offer the male assistance in walking down the sandy hill. Thus far, Noah had seemed unable to see where to place his feet. "I do apologize, Noah."

"For what?"

"That I was unable to devote myself to healing your eyes completely in one session. I did not feel able to delay, and to give more energy to the act would have compromised my—"

"It's fine, Vivek. I can handle this."

Vivek smiled at him when they reached the bottom of the hill. "You are quite resilient."

"Don't have much choice." Noah shrugged and took Bendel back.

Vivek kept his resultant thought of Noah's bravery to himself and simply led him toward the market. Noah might think his choice to move forward come what may an easy one to make, but Vivek had been there when people he thought were courageous saw such futility in struggle that they succumbed instead. Escaping Tev was not a war, but for Noah, it might as well be—capture now would most likely mean death. Vivek admired Noah's fortitude.

As they entered an aisle between stalls, Vivek realized vendors watched them curiously. He had been prepared for the scene he might cause since it was impossible to disguise that he was Aguadite, but their onlookers seemed most curious about Noah...and Bendel. Whispered conversation speculated on what afflicted the child.

While Noah's wrapping of Bendel was efficient, apparently, it gave a poor impression of Bendel's health. The appearance of illness would not secure them passage on any ship, and the deepness of Bendel's slumber might even make him appear deceased.

"Noah?"

"Yeah?" He focused on Vivek's face. "Is something wrong?" he whispered.

"Bendel seems to be causing a ripple of curiosity."

Noah looked down at the bundled child, and then loosened the blankets around his face. "Should I unwrap him? He does look...curious, I guess."

"Finding him clothing and giving the appearance of a napping child would be better."

"Should you wake him up?"

"No," Vivek said and looked for a clothing stall selling small, bipedal sizes. "It would take too much of my energy to do so now."

Noah's head snapped up and those clouded eyes searched Vivek's face. "What do you need?" he asked. "I don't want you collapsing or something." His fist crushed a portion of Vivek's vest.

His concern was touching. When was the last time someone had cared? "Easy," Vivek said and stroked the side of Noah's neck. "I need to sleep, then eat, and can only do that once I know we are secure on a ship. I am well, Noah. Do not worry."

"Okay. All right," Noah said, but his pulse was fast against Vivek's fingertips. "Let's just get started. Give me something to do."

If being busy would help Noah remain at ease, Vivek could accommodate him. He led him toward a clothing stall. While Vivek explained to the Palocam vendor that Bendel was exhausted and recently purchased, Noah unwrapped the child. He seemed reluctant to let the vendor touch Bendel.

"My slave here," Vivek said, inwardly cringing over the word. "He will assist you in dressing the youth while I obtain food stuffs. He does not speak Tok."

"We will work together," they said in agreement before turning to select a small purple shirt and black pants.

To Noah he said, "Get two shirts, one pair of pants, and boots. Make sure everything fits and is clean. I will be behind you at a stall or two collecting food and water. Remain here until I return."

Noah swallowed hard, looked away, and then back. "Just don't take too long, okay?"

"I will be quick." Vivek could not resist touching Noah's shoulder, offering reassurance. "If anyone approaches you, say *boktig*. That means 'owned slave' and they will leave you alone."

Noah blew out a breath as he took the shirt he'd given Bendel off of his limp little body. "*Boktig*. Got it."

"I will watch over your slaves," the vendor said and pounded a fist on the table in a typical Palocam show of commitment. The move made Noah jump.

"This guy isn't Human, is he? I mean he looks it, but like a Human hopped up on a shit-ton of steroids and grown hormones, but still. Not Human, right?"

"No, they are not Human."

"They?"

"I would not presume to label their gender."

Noah's brief, sharp laugh sounded tense. "Yeah, okay."

"I will return shortly," he said to the Palocam vendor, and then repeated it to Noah with a pat to his back.

Vivek turned to the stalls behind him. He recognized a few of the fruits on his own, got recommendations on the protein products, and managed to purchase long-travel containers for everything as well. No fish of any kind—he dearly missed the sustenance of the ocean. Water was a little harder to come by since the Tevian needed very little of it and non-Tevian vendors were few of late—the Palocam was one of only three here today. But, after demonstrating how much he was willing to pay for water, two vendors handed over their own containers. Thankfully, the entire process took hardly any time at all.

When Vivek returned, it was to see Noah smiling at Bendel hanging limply from Noah's hold under his spindly arms while the Palocam finished tugging a pair of pants up Bendel's legs. Vivek winced when they did not adjust the cloth before yanking it over Bendel's little genitals. Vivek walked over with his two bags of supplies as Noah lay Bendel on the table and adjusted his pants, mumbling apologies.

Vivek had to wonder if Noah might be a parent given their discussion about modifications and his demonstrated care for Bendel. Suddenly, the greatness of Noah's losses put a weight in Vivek's chest. Could they return Noah to his family? He knew there was an organization called the Earth Campaign, but did not know exactly what they did for Humans or how to make contact with them. He would double his efforts to see that Noah connected with the group once they were safely in Coalition space.

He smiled at Noah's attempts to get Bendel's feet into a pair of boots. The vendor tried to help, but their hands were too large to do much more than hold Bendel's leg steady. Bendel gave a great snore just as Noah got one boot on him.

Suddenly, a bright beam of sunlight cut through a space between the tents above them. They needed to keep moving. No doubt, by now, someone had noticed several sleeping guards, if not two escaped prisoners.

"Noah, we must leave."

"Okay. He looks good, right?" He propped Bendel up and rubbed at a smudge on the child's cheek. "A little grubby, but kids get like that. We shouldn't have a problem now, right?" His voice was high, tense.

"No, no difficulties. You have done well." Vivek offered his hand so the vendor could scan it for a credit transfer and rubbed Noah's back at the same time. Noah folded the blankets with jerky movements. "There is room in this bag for those."

"Should I carry everything?" Noah ask quietly, indicating the bags.

"Technically, yes."

"Hand them over, then. If I'm going to play a slave, I'm going to play a good one."

Vivek gave up the bags, helping to get them onto one of Noah's broad shoulders so he could carry Bendel against the other. Looking at Noah now, Vivek realized a great deal of the male's pale skin was available to the sun.

"Noah, does sunlight have an adverse effect on your skin?"

"If I'm out in it long enough, yeah. Why?"

Vivek took his thin, black cloak out of the pocket on his thigh and put it around Noah's shoulders, draping it to cover Bendel as well. "The intensity of the sunlight here is quite high. What might have been 'long enough' on Earth could prove a much shorter span here." He secured the catch at the neck and flipped the hood up over Noah's head. "The hood will also provide some shade for your eyes."

Noah released the strap of one bag to catch Vivek's hand and squeeze it. "Thank you," he said, his voice rough.

Vivek smiled and placed his hand against the small of Noah's back as he steered them toward the ship recruiters.

CHAPTER THIRTEEN

The sun scorched the transport hub with increasingly harsh golden light as Vivek led the way through the much more diverse crowd. Traders from many different planets hocked their goods from stalls set up in the open bays of the shuttles nearest the market. Vivek did not even recognize some of the species he saw and he was quite knowledgeable in that area. At any other time, he might have questioned the people, learned about them, but urgency to escape moved him onward.

"They're all so small," Noah said beside him as he squinted under his hood.

"What are?"

"The ships. Barely bigger than mine was."

"These are transport shuttles that will take us to the ships in orbit."

"Oh, right. Of course. We did that, too."

Vivek wanted to ask Noah about Earth's travel capabilities given Noah's awed expression, but he did not wish to bring them additional attention. Most owners did not converse with their slaves. Many more eyes watched them closely now, no doubt in an effort to gauge their business, worth, or vulnerabilities. Vivek refocused on his task of finding them a way off-planet.

Eventually, the hub catered more to recruiters looking for passengers or crew. They called out the models and amenities of their ships, promised speed or discretion, and some gave incentives like free meals or sexual partners.

"Are you in need of transport?" someone asked in Bedelso, the most common language even this far out.

Vivek stopped and looked over a nude male with ruddy red skin and large black eyes. He looked like he might be part of the Helokis species, but there was something rather reptilian about him.

"I do," Vivek answered. "Do you have room for three passengers?"

"We may. Is that one a sex worker?" He nodded at Noah.

Vivek looked over at Noah. He was a very handsome male and obviously fit. Was Noah a passionate lover? Would he be aggressive and dominant to regain some of the control he did not have now? *Inappropriate and ill-timed*, he chided himself. Vivek turned back to the recruiter.

"No, he is not a sex worker."

"Trade it to me and I will transport you anywhere you—"

"I have ample credits to pay for our passage."

"Credits are fine, but sexual diversions are more—"

Vivek took hold of Noah's arm and walked them

away. They had other options. He also did not wish to analyze why he suddenly felt so possessive of Noah.

"What's wrong?" Noah asked as he stumbled to keep up.

Vivek steadied Noah and slowed their pace. "He was unwilling to negotiate with me." He did not need to burden Noah with the rest.

"Well, there's plenty more to choose from."

"Exactly."

They walked on.

Vivek avoided a group of Golson with their four hoofed feet, muscular arms, and pale green skin getting slowly darker from the sun. He could not trust them. Were they here because they knew of the impending alliance? Vivek guided Noah far from them.

An Obelio female with thick white hair down to her thighs and a pair of enormous red and white feathered wings on her back smiled at him. He stopped to speak with her.

"Are you accepting passengers?"

"We are, though we fly toward Trizeylia first."

"That is acceptable." Trizeylia was a colonized moon near a controlled tri-portal that would get them into Coalition space much faster than simple flight. "What is the cost for three?"

"I could use a healer. Are you available?"

Why was no one interested in his credits?

"I am contracted." It was the easiest lie and something most understood since it conveyed both the expensive nature of his services and the fact he was not available to anyone but the contract holder.

"Pity." She turned away.

Vivek stalked onward only to have Noah grab at him. He stopped to explain. "She refused—"

"Not that. I can't *see.*"

Vivek stepped closer and peered under the hood covering half of Noah's face. Even that hidden in shadow, the sunlight was still strong enough to have tears cascading down his cheeks from the ocular irritation.

He dragged Noah beneath an overlap of shuttle wings, and then blocked the sun from reflecting off the sand at their feet by standing close to him. Through it all, Bendel still slept peacefully on Noah's shoulder beneath the cloak.

"I apologize." Vivek gently wiped the tears from Noah's face. "I did not realize you suffered so."

"It's all right. It doesn't hurt, I just couldn't see you."

Vivek cupped Noah's face and inspected the still-murky eyes trying to see him. Losing sight of Vivek had frightened Noah a great deal. It occurred to Vivek then how Noah might see him as his only link to survival.

"I will afford you greater attention from now on, Noah."

"Okay." He nodded into Vivek's hands, taking deep breaths.

Vivek kept one hand on Noah's jaw and took the supply bags with the other. "Hold onto Bendel and close your eyes. I will guide you."

"How about this?" He wrapped his fingers around Vivek's upper arm, near his elbow. "I'll just hold onto you."

"Yes, very well." He could not physically react to it

because of the *alinex* he'd taken, but he knew he liked having Noah's long fingers touching the bare skin of his arm. The contrast between his gray and Noah's pale pink was rather lovely as well.

Vivek looked away and noticed a large, male Krittikan observing them. At least a head and a half taller than Vivek, the Krittikan was covered in short fur with a thick mane of equally dark brown. His golden, vertically slit eyes locked onto Vivek and he stared. Vivek walked over.

In Kretch, the native tongue on Krittika, Vivek asked, "Are you taking on passengers?"

"I am." He nodded his head toward Noah and Bendel. "Are they healthy?"

"Yes, of course. The young one is merely exhausted from the auction." Assuming there had been one already today. "The other has sensitive eyes unused to this harsh sunlight."

The Krittikan nodded and hummed. "I can understand that." He tapped his temple, probably indicating the artificial lenses darkening the gold color of his eyes. "The crew is all Krittikan, so the ship has lower lighting. It will be good for him."

Hope built inside Vivek. "Do you have room for us then?"

The Krittikan stepped into Vivek's space to say, "I do not abide slavery."

Vivek took another chance and smiled. "Neither do I."

He lay his fingers over Noah's on his arm and patted them. With perfect timing, Noah moved closer to Vivek, brushing his chest against Vivek's back. Hopefully, the Krittikan would see either someone rescuing slaves or someone needing the ruse of owning them. There might be more discussion later, but it would be off-planet and Vivek had no problem explaining his rescue efforts then.

The Krittikan nodded. "I am Captain Dezon Malcree. We journey into Coalition space, though we will stop on Maura for fresh supplies."

It was excellent that they traveled into Coalition space, but Vivek had never heard of that planet. Not that he knew all of them, but he was aware of the nearby trade routes. "Maura?"

"An abandoned Golson outpost left over from the Krittikan Revolution." Malcree stared into Vivek's eyes, his feline face giving nothing away. "I hear Maura delegates are attempting to enter the Coalition right now."

Vivek understood. This Krittikan was against slavery and a loyalist to his homeworld, a place that had only thrown off the yolk of Golson rule a mere ten cycles ago. He was testing Vivek, and no wonder, given the Golson activity here on Tev.

If he only knew what Vivek knew.

"Any planet is better than here," Vivek said. "Perhaps once we arrive on Maura, we will hear of their success. I would welcome a reason to celebrate."

Nodding with a small smile, Captain Malcree brought out his credit scanner. "Two thousand each for you and the pale one. Eight hundred for the child. One of you will accompany him whenever he leaves your berth."

"Of course. Agreed."

After mutually approving the total of the transaction and seeing confirmation, the captain smiled, fangs gleaming, and gestured toward the shuttle behind him. "Welcome aboard the *Windfall Drift*. Please find seats inside, secure yourselves, and we will take off as soon as the last member of my crew returns."

Vivek stepped into the open shuttle via its rear ramp and felt a blessed end to the scorching sun. While his skin could take the rays, he preferred a cooler, moister climate. In addition to the lower lighting for Noah, it was possible a Krittikan crew would keep their ship's environment at a milder temperature as well. Vivek felt a great deal of tension leave his body as he set down their packs and helped Noah into a jump seat.

"So we're okay?" Noah whispered, eyes wide open again. "We're going with him?"

"Yes, everything is acceptable." Vivek took Bendel and put him in a seat with a bag on either side propping him up before strapping him in. "Be cautious, of course, but I am hopeful."

"Good. Okay." Noah took a series of deep breaths for a moment. He pushed the hood back and ran his hands through the dark hair on his head. His hands shook.

"Your nose is very red," Vivek said with some concern as he bound Noah's torso to his seat.

Noah touched his nose and winced. "Sunburn. It's fine."

"I will heal it—"

"*No*, save your strength."

"—Later," he finished and smiled. "Worry not, Noah. I am tired, but well."

"Okay."

"Okay," Vivek echoed, liking that word for its many uses.

He took a seat beside Noah and strapped himself in. In the interest of allaying any possible fears Noah might have regarding spaceflight, Vivek explained what would soon happen.

"There may be a great deal of vibration as we leave the atmosphere—it depends on the pilot's skills and the capabilities of the shuttle. We will also experience weightlessness until we dock with the ship."

"The ship'll have gravity?" Noah seemed quite surprised.

"It will. Your ships do not?"

"No, they don't," Noah said. "We were weightless until they captured us and brought us inside their ship." He closed his eyes and swallowed hard before ducking his head.

"How did you manage to travel so far from Earth without gravity?"

Noah looked up. "A wormhole. It sucked us in and..." He cleared his throat and shifted until their shoulders pressed together. "I flew a small ship back and forth between Earth and our moon all the time, but that wormhole was never there before. It suddenly hit us and..." He shrugged and swallowed hard.

Vivek was unsure whether Noah's wormhole was the same as an unstable portal, but he suspected as much. He reached over and held Noah's hand. Noah squeezed, their palms pressing tight. It was an intimate and telling hold, though Vivek was unsure if Noah knew that. Vivek let it be since he drew comfort from the connection as well.

A younger, leaner Krittikan dashed through the shuttle and up a small flight of stairs into the cockpit. Moments later, Captain Malcree walked by and smiled with a nod toward Vivek and Noah. *Interesting.* Krittikan had strict rules regarding physical interactions. If Vivek was not mistaken, to a Krittikan, a public display such as holding hands would mean he and Noah were mate-bonded. That could be advantageous.

Vivek squeezed Noah's hand briefly. He leaned back to wait for their take-off with a pleasant sense of accomplishment and anticipation coursing through him.

CHAPTER FOURTEEN

ANOTHER DAMN ALIEN SHIP

Noah kept an eye on Vivek through the flight away from the planet. He might not be able to see him very well, but he could tell Vivek was heading for a crash. Given the number of times he seemed to shake himself awake while they sat there, Noah was pretty sure Vivek was nearing complete exhaustion.

It worried him. He needed Vivek to lead for more reasons than just that Vivek could see better. Noah didn't know the language that big blur of a guy had spoken, he didn't have whatever it was in his hand that let Vivek pay for things, and he had absolutely no idea where to go or what to do from one minute to the next. Yes, by damn, he hated being so helpless and useless and beholden to another person, but Noah couldn't do this on his own.

Sweat beaded on his upper lip. He swiped it away. When he realized his knee was bouncing, he tried to sit still. He'd been slowly freaking out since they'd sealed the hatch. Though the takeoff had been smoother than anything he had ever known, it was still heading back up into space inside a tiny can. He didn't want to stay on that hell planet, but sweet Christ...

"It is a decent ship," Vivek said beside him. "More bulky freighter than sleek passenger ship, but it looks well-maintained. One visible gun turret which makes me think it may be fast enough to avoid a fight. That is good."

Noah knew what Vivek was trying to do for him. He gave their clasped hands a squeeze and tried to let Vivek's low voice soothe him. But it was Vivek's face, so close for the first time, that distracted Noah.

Vivek's dove gray skin had an undertone of pale pink and slightly darker stripes accentuating his features. His head was rounded on top, but with a square jaw. This close up, Noah could see Vivek's pupils were large and black, not his entire eye, because there was a thin ring of silver around them. And even as foreign as Vivek's face was with barely any nose and those eyes so far apart, the plump bottom lip and how quick Vivek was to smile reassurance made him intriguingly handsome.

Noah jumped in his seat when the shuttle banged down, stopped moving. Along with a hiss of pressurization they regained gravity. Bile rose in Noah's throat, making him swallow convulsively. He would *not* lose it. Not here. Not now.

"All is well." Vivek stroked the back of his fingers against Noah's cheek. "We have docked with the ship and will now find our berth for the remainder of our journey."

Taking deep breaths, Noah nodded. After Vivek unstrapped him, he made himself stand up, put his arms out, and accept Bendel when Vivek offered him. *Keep it together*.

Noah concentrated on following Vivek's black clothing through the dimly lit, gray corridors. The big guy Vivek had negotiated with babbled at them the whole way. There was something disturbingly familiar to the way the alien spoke. It made Noah even twitchier.

When they all stopped, the alien slid open a door of orange panels to reveal a golden-hued light inside a small room. As far as Noah could see, though, the room was empty.

The alien leaned past Noah, gesturing into the room. With a gasp of recognition, Noah flinched back, clutching Bendel to his chest. The bastard was one of the lion-men? *Shit. Shit!* Heart pounding, head buzzing, Noah stumbled away. He bumped Vivek, who grabbed his arm.

"Noah?"

"It's..." He could barely get the words out. "It's one... It's one of *them*."

"Who?"

"That fucking alien. Keep it *away* from me!"

Vivek held onto Noah's upper arms and got close to his face. "Why do you fear him so?"

"One of those fuckers blinded me. Took away my crew." He gulped in between panted breaths. "Vivek, we have to *get out of here*."

Vivek shook his head. "Captain Malcree will not harm you like that other did. They may be the same race, but they are not of the same beliefs. Please allow for that."

Noah shook his head. "You tell— You tell him what they did to me."

Nodding, Vivek rubbed up and down Noah's arms while he spoke. It was that Russian-sounding language he'd heard on the ship that captured him and his crew. When the guy let loose a string of hard sounds, Noah couldn't help flinching away. Vivek looped one arm around behind him, though, and Noah found himself leaning into the solid strength of him.

"He understands your trepidation," Vivek said, "and wishes you to know he is most definitely *not* like those you have encountered. The drug used to blind you is something he is familiar with and very much against. I am sure you heard his tone."

"Sure. Okay."

He knew he was being prejudiced—he did—but, damn it, so far he had exactly one person he could trust. Maybe he could trust Bendel, but it was still possible the kid had manipulated him from the start. Vivek was it for him.

The lion-man said something more before Vivek said, "He says he will request that his crew keep their distance from you, but he would like the opportunity to demonstrate their differing views."

"Whatever, just...later, all right?" He needed some room to breathe for a while.

"Of course." Vivek spoke again to— Well, apparently he was the captain. After a few more quiet but intense words, the lion-man walked away.

Vivek entered the small room. "I can promise you, Noah, that he is most definitely not like the Krittikan you met. There are two factions as a result of war on their planet—those who view you and I as quite inferior and those who see us all as equals. Captain Malcree belongs to the latter group."

Noah only nodded. He'd think about it.

Vivek fiddled with something on the far wall before lowering down...the wall? As Vivek stepped out of the room, Noah realized it was a platform that snapped into place about two feet off the floor and filled the small room.

Noah set Bendel down on the mattress. "So this is our berth for the trip?"

"Yes. There are seats that can fold down instead, but I must rest."

"Right. Yeah. Get in there and sleep."

Vivek climbed in. "Noah, I must—"

"No, it's okay."

Vivek got about half-way inside before he just collapsed. It seemed involuntary given his grunt and struggle to keep going. "But you need—"

"I need you well-rested and ready to go when we land or whatever happens next." He crawled in and leaned over Vivek. Noah touched Vivek's forehead, encouraging him to put his head down. "Just sleep. I'll stay right here with you. Don't worry."

Vivek sighed, closed his eyes, and dropped off that fast. Noah had a moment to realize Vivek must trust him, too.

He pulled Vivek the rest of the way into room and away from the door. He went back and hauled Bendel near the top of the bed since he was little. Finally, Noah slid the door shut, hoping the beep signaled it was latched. He sat there staring through dim golden lighting and blurry eyes at the one person he desperately needed.

He was no better than a child out here. Well, no, Bendel was probably more experienced just by not being Human. Noah was completely ill-equipped to handle even the most basic aspects of the world around him. He *needed* Vivek. He couldn't do *any* of this without Vivek.

Trying to breathe through rising panic and talk himself down—because, rationally, he knew there really was no reason to freak since Vivek was *asleep, not dead*—Noah hunkered down on the thin mattress close to Vivek.

He wouldn't sleep. He'd stayed awake for a couple of days before, so he could do it now. If he slept, he might go under too deep and miss something. Someone had to look out for Vivek while he recharged. Bendel couldn't help. It was down to the mostly blind guy who didn't have a goddamned clue what he was doing.

Noah curled over his knees and held on tight.

CHAPTER FIFTEEN

N oah opened his eyes to see the pale orange ceiling of their berth. *Shit!* He'd slept. He looked around. Vivek was gone.

"*Vivek?*"

"It's all right," Bendel said from near his feet. "He's gone to get more water."

Heart hammering, Noah looked the kid over as he moved to sit beside him and try to calm down again. *No reason to panic.* If Vivek was up and fetching water, it meant he felt better. *See? Everything's fine.*

Bendel had parted his dark hair down the center of his little head and woven into two braids. Noah tucked a wisp behind Bendel's ear as the kid grinned at him. "You look a lot better," Noah said.

"I *feel* better." Bendel wrapped both his arms around Noah's one and squeezed. "Thank you so much for rescuing me."

Noah untangled his arm and gave him a proper hug and back rub. "Thank *you* for giving me that sight thing."

He suddenly decided he didn't care about the emotional manipulation. He'd have done the same thing, if he could've. Bendel wasn't at fault there.

"Vivek can heal your eyes more, yes?" Bendel reached up and touched Noah's cheek for a moment.

Noah glanced out through the partially open door into a monochrome room. "He said he would as soon as he was able. He used a lot of his own energy on us yesterday."

"He is quite selfless."

Noah nodded agreement and kept his eyes on the featureless space outside their bunk, waiting for a gray blob wearing black to appear and come back to him.

Come back to me? Noah rubbed at his eyes. He really needed to get a grip.

"Vivek said we could investigate the facilities after you ate." Bendel scratched at his scalp. "I am desperate for a bath."

"Oh, me, too. And a toilet."

"That's in there," Bendel said and pointed at the wall across from their bunk. "Can you see it?"

"Probably once I get closer." Noah scooted to the edge and swung his legs over the side of the bunk and into the hall. He looked left and right, feeling like he might be breaking a rule by getting up. Since there was nothing but gray with either light or shadow, he stood and shuffled over to the wall with both hands out.

"The yellow sticker is where the handle is," Bendel said behind him. "Put your fingers under it and pull out."

Noah could see the yellow now, so he opened the

narrow door outward. A dim light flickered on inside a tiny room. Was it like on his ship with hoses and—

"No, it's like you knew on Earth. You can simply sit down."

He looked back at Bendel. "What?"

"It's an actual toilet. Well, mostly. Neither it nor the sink use water. Put your hands in the sink and a beam of light will clean them."

Noah took a breath and let it out. "I'm going to do this, then we're going to talk about that mental eavesdropping you're doing."

"Oh. Yes, okay."

Noah went inside the tiny room and shut the door behind himself. Pissing while holding his dress up was oh so much fun. Was his slave status over? That would be nice, but he probably had to check in with Vivek first. Was Bendel out there wondering about it with him? Maybe the kid was polite enough not to dig around in his head all the time.

Finished and washed up—or as clean as a blue light was going to get him—Noah left the bathroom and climbed back up onto the bunk feeling a lot more stable. That had been what he'd needed, normalcy, a familiar routine of any kind.

"Vivek said there should be a cleanser on board somewhere and he'd find it for us." Bendel fidgeted, crossing and then straightening out his legs.

"Yeah, all right, but... Kid, I need you to quit reading my mind, okay?"

"It's not mind-reading. Your subconscious likes to share and, sometimes, it's loud about it." He looked at him, and Noah could just make out the concerned expression. "I can't hear everything all the time. Only the...important stuff. I will only speak to you telepathically in emergencies."

"Okay. That I can understand and deal with. Just don't go fishing in here," he said and tapped his temple.

"Promise." He leaned forward and grabbed something that looked like a dark green orange. "Here, eat this. It's good."

Noah held the weird food. How was he supposed to eat it? The sting of needing assistance bit him again. "What do I do with it?"

"Just bite it," Bendel said. "Don't eat the seed in the middle."

The pebbled skin was a bit chewy and the fruit had the consistency of ripe avocado, but it tasted like a peach. "This *is* good."

"I don't know what it is, but I liked it, too."

"Well, that's something at least."

"What is?"

Noah felt his cheeks heating. "It's nice to know I'm not the only one who's really out of his element right now."

"It has been a long time since I last left my planet." Bendel patted Noah's knee. "Many things are very different from before. We will learn them together."

Noah swallowed a mouthful. "How could it have been a long time? You're just a kid."

His eyes weren't so bad that he couldn't recognize someone who'd given away more than he'd meant to.

Bendel looked down at his lap. "I... I would prefer not to explain right now."

Secrets. Wasn't a bad thing, technically. They barely knew each other and, yeah, Bendel was the more vulnerable. Unless he had some kind of superpower like Vivek, the kid could keep his secrets until he felt safe enough to share.

"Sure, kid. No problem."

After Noah finished his not-a-peach, Bendel was showing Noah where to ditch the fruit's pit when someone large and mostly brown passed by their doorway. Noah and Bendel both froze, but the lion-man kept walking. As Noah let the pit drop down the waste chute built into the wall, Bendel leaned out the door.

Suddenly, Noah heard Vivek's voice. He didn't understand the words he said, but Bendel smiled as he scooted back into the berth. Pushing the door open more, Noah watched the pale gray and black shape of Vivek come closer. Relief washed through him.

When Vivek got to them he was smiling. He leaned over and set three small, white things down on the floor, and then held a hand out to Noah. "Come out here."

Noah took his hand, and Vivek gave it an encouraging tug. Noah lunged out of the berth and hugged Vivek tightly. *What am I doing?* But then Vivek wrapped his arms around him in return and squeezed. Noah sighed.

"Are you well, Noah?"

He pulled back, his face hot. "Yes, fine. Just...glad you're back."

"I apologize for leaving while you slept, but without

my energy fortifying you, your body will require sustenance." Vivek bent to retrieve one of the white things—was it seriously a teapot?—and gave it to Noah. "Bendel and I drank all the water without realizing, so this is yours. Pull this back and tip it up."

Glad for the direction, Noah did so and drank from the spout while Vivek got Bendel and all their things out of the berth. The water tasted a little metallic, but it was wet and clean so it was good. He drank the whole pot.

Vivek refastened the bunk to the wall and dropped down a long bench from the underside of it. On the opposite wall and beside the door, Vivek folded down two cushioned seats. They stored their supplies in a corner beside the chairs and away from the door. Noah sat on the bench, while Bendel took a chair. Vivek closed the door until it beeped.

"Did you eat?" Vivek sat in the other chair.

"Yes," Bendel said. "We had some fruit."

"Typical youth." Vivek booped Bendel's button nose. "Did you eat any protein at all?"

Bendel pulled the bag around, closer to Vivek. "I am unfamiliar with most of these items."

"Ah. My apologies." Vivek reached into the bag and pulled out a tied sack. "These are a variation of the almond nuts native to Conlani."

Noah frowned. "We have almonds on *Earth*."

Bendel stuffed a bunch of them in his mouth as Vivek said, "This does not surprise me. There are those who believe an ancient people once populated the habitable worlds of the universe with genetic material from their home world. It explains why there are so many similarities in flora and fauna."

Noah let his head drop back against the wall with a thump. Ancient aliens populated the universe? Like some kind of science project? Playing at being a god? On one hand that would explain the whole species versus races thing Vivek had mentioned before, but on the other that was just...*whoa*. Was Earth not the native planet for humans?

Before Noah could lose his mind over that, Vivek knelt on the floor beside him.

"I would like to heal your eyes more—or possibly completely—and then transfer my knowledge of a few languages to you. Is this acceptable?"

Noah flinched back. "What? Fuck, no." He lunged for the door, heart hammering.

"Noah?"

In the hall, Noah couldn't see shit. And where the hell was he going to go anyway.

"You are *not* going to use one of those brain burners on me," he said when Vivek's blurry shape came closer. "Absolutely no fucking way. You hear me?"

"I do not understand what you mean by brain burners." Vivek stayed back, but he kept reaching and withdrawing, too.

"Stop that." Noah smacked at Vivek's hand.

"Noah, I do not understand your anger toward me. What have I done?"

"Those gooey things with tentacles that makes my whole head feel like it's on fire—that's a brain burner." He shook with the memories. "It took the language right out of my head and gave it to the son of a bitch who ate it. They goddamn *tortured* me with it. Over and over."

Noah stepped closer, tense, ready to fight and so damn disappointed. "How could you do that to me? To anyone?"

Vivek stepped in fast and close, grabbing Noah's wrists and immobilizing him. Noah gasped, struggled, and Vivek pressed him back against the wall.

"Look at me," Vivek said. "Look at me and hear me, Noah. I would never use such a heinous creature on you or anyone else. Never. They are illegal, dangerous, and horrific."

Noah stared at Vivek's face and saw the shock and sincerity. "Oh, goddamn. Of course, you... *You* wouldn't use that." He closed his eyes and gulped, sagging back against the wall. "Vivek, I'm sorry."

Vivek let Noah's wrists go, but then Noah found himself wrapped up in Vivek's arms. It felt like a protective embrace, Vivek holding Noah close and tight. A tremor ran through Vivek.

"I share languages in the same manner that I heal," Vivek whispered. "It is energy, nothing harmful. I could *never...*"

"I know," Noah whispered back. "I freaked. I'm—"

"Understandable." Vivek stepped back, but kept ahold of Noah's shoulders. "With your permission, I would like to check for and heal any damage the hodorite might have done, as well as heal your eyes and transfer the languages."

Noah nodded. "Yeah. Okay." He sighed. "Okay."

Vivek guided Noah back into their berth. Bendel

gave Noah's hand a squeeze as Noah walked toward the bench against the wall. He gave the kid a smile and sat down heavily.

"Lay back," Vivek said quietly. "And I need access to your skin."

Noah stretched out on the bench, and Vivek snaked one hand down the top of Noah's dress. Vivek's warm palm rested between Noah's pecs. Vivek's other hand cradled the back of Noah's neck. Held again. Wasn't a bad thing at all. Coming down off the adrenaline rush had left him shaky. He tried to relax.

"By the way," Vivek said, "we may be able to procure new clothing for you."

"Something that isn't a dress?" Noah asked with a smile while trying to ignore the zing of Vivek's hands on him.

"Something not a dress." Vivek grinned and closed his eyes. "Lay still and quiet for me, Noah. You will feel heat from my hands that will travel to your eyes. It will not hurt. You may feel a pleasant sort of contentment."

Noah closed his eyes, too, feeling that warmth spreading up from his chest to merge with the same in his neck. Heat blossomed in his head, he could feel it in his eyes, and it wasn't just contentment he felt. Sexual need took him by surprise. He opened his mouth, moaning before he could stop himself. The arousing sensation went on and on, flowing all through him.

Noah felt Vivek panting against his collarbone. Vivek's broad, square palm shook a little as he cupped the base of Noah's head. "Blessed spirits," Vivek whispered.

The warming sensation dissipated back down to its starting points.

Noah knew those words Vivek had spoken hadn't been English. He didn't know what language it was, but it was new to him. He opened his mouth to say something, and found himself speaking the same language back. "Are you...well?" There was no word for *all right* or *okay*. He moved his arm to rest a hand on the small of Vivek's back, felt the muscles there jump as Vivek's breath hitched.

"Your eyes," Vivek said, and then swallowed hard. "Your eyes should be clearer now."

Clear enough he could see the lust in Vivek's expression. He'd felt the same thing Noah had. Vivek's black eyes focus in on Noah's mouth. Vivek leaned closer. Noah licked his lips, and Vivek's pink tongue slid out to wet his own plump bottom lip. Noah smiled, and Vivek's gaze snapped up to his eyes. He looked so unsure.

Whispering in that same new language, Noah asked, "Do you want to kiss me?"

"You do that?"

Noah cupped the back of Vivek's smooth head. Vivek shivered as Noah pulled him closer. Vivek's eyelids closed and his warm, sweet breath washed Noah's face. Soft, lush lips lightly pressed to his.

The kiss was so tentative. Noah let Vivek kiss him like that, gentle presses and tiny rubs, wondering if this was his first one. As charming as that was, he hoped it wasn't the case. If Vivek didn't know what sex was like for an Aguadite, that would make two of them.

Vivek's tongue peeked out and traced Noah's upper

lip. He opened for it, wanting to pull Vivek down, plunder and taste. Vivek gave a quiet moan and did lean over Noah more, did slip that tongue in to caress his. He moaned his approval right back, tipping his chin up to ask for even more. And then he realized Vivek was *not* new at this. All that innocence had been a tease. Vivek was a *very* good kisser.

A beep startled them apart, both now looking to the door. It was closed. Had someone— Vivek stood up.

"I apologize," he said. "I— He cannot—" Vivek glanced down Noah's body, cleared his throat, and then lunged toward the door.

Still a little dazed, Noah looked himself over. He groaned. His erection was pushing up his damn dress. He sat up and bloused the cloth around his waist to hide it while he listened to Vivek and Bendel.

Out in the hall, Vivek said, "Bendel, you cannot leave."

"I am giving you privacy."

"I apologize for...indulging. I should not have done that."

Vivek *didn't* want to kiss him? While that helped cool the problem throbbing between Noah's legs, it bit into his self-esteem, too. It had felt like Vivek wanted him, but maybe kissing meant something else to his people? Ridiculous, but maybe.

"It looked to me," Bendel said, "like you both wanted to...indulge."

Vivek made a quiet, squawking noise before his voice was more firm. "Bendel, the captain expressly forbade me to allow you out of our berth without a chaperone. You are too young to be on your own."

Bendel's snort was amused, but they both came back into the small room. Bendel waggled his little eyebrows at Noah before he hopped into a chair again. Noah shook his head and grinned back, certain now something was going on with Bendel; he seemed way older than he looked. And since he was an alien...

Vivek stood awkwardly in the doorway. Noah took pity on him. Besides, if Vivek didn't want to "indulge" with him, Noah didn't want to know why while Bendel was there. He'd see about catching Vivek alone later. If nothing else, he didn't want to offend his main link to survival.

"What language is this?" Noah asked in the same language Vivek had used when he whispered about spirits while healing him.

Vivek nodded and came inside to sit in the other chair. He handed Bendel the bag of almonds again, looked at the floor by his long feet. "It is...my own people's language. Sowasish." The skin of his thick neck and up into his cheeks turned a deep pink.

Noah couldn't help smiling. "And which one is this?" Noah asked, since it wasn't English.

"Bedelso. Even on Tev, where we were, they speak it well enough." Vivek's next words weren't in Bedelso. "Once we leave the ship, you will likely not need Kretch as often. I felt it would be helpful while here, given your previous reaction to the captain."

Noah nodded. "Yes, it will...ease my mind. It is a rather formal language for all the harsh sounds." It felt a bit like he might go hoarse from the throaty noises he had to make. It was amazing how it felt natural to speak Kretch. He only had to pause to find a word or phrase equivalent to the English slang he wanted to use.

"Why did you give Sowasish to me?" Noah asked, using the rather lyrical language. "Are we likely to encounter more Aguadite soon?"

Vivek's previously fading blush renewed. "No." He opened his mouth as if to say more, but then only cleared his throat and fidgeted with a pocket on his pant leg.

"Another indulgence?" Noah whispered with a small grin.

Despite leaving Bendel out of the conversation by speaking Sowasish, the kid giggled when Vivek sat back and crossed his legs and arms very much like he planned to sit there and pout. Noah chuckled, too, and then Vivek broke and grinned through more blushing. He grabbed a handful of almonds from Bendel's bag and tossed them at Noah. About ten of them landed in the hammock of Noah's skirt between his knees, while a couple pinged off his chest to hit the floor.

"Eat your protein," Vivek grumbled.

"As you wish." Noah made sure he had Vivek's gaze when he used his tongue to catch an almond from his palm.

Vivek gave Noah a pretty promising smile.

CHAPTER SIXTEEN

All of them now fed and adapted, Vivek led them from their berth to find and use the passenger facilities. Thankfully, it was closer than the mess had been when he went to find drinking water; the bathing chambers were literally around the corner. No other passengers were present—if there even were any others aboard—so Vivek took his time explaining to both his charges how to use the various devices within.

Once Noah and Bendel were enclosed in their own compartments, Vivek entered the last one and tried to press upon himself that one did not seduce one's innocent and dependent... Traveling companion? Refugee? Regardless, he should not have indulged despite Noah's obvious desire and later flirtations. It would be wrong to take advantage of Noah's situation.

Vivek undressed and arranged his clothing in the slot that would clean them in the same fashion as his skin. The evidence of his arousal had faded, though the sensation that it could return with a few thoughts made him focus on submitting to the cleanser. To merely relax and accept the warm lights and bursts of air as they swirled around him. Later, he would take more *alinex* and mute his sexual impulses again.

But his mind flashed back to the flush of want on Noah's face after Vivek kissed him.

He had felt Noah's near instant arousal as soon as the healing commenced. The reaction was unusual, not one Vivek had ever encountered during his training or afterward. But the sensation had been as though Noah's body gave back to Vivek in joyous thanks for his intervention. He healed, and Noah rewarded. Deliciously. That had not happened in the dungeon when Noah had been unconscious while Vivek healed him. This time had been exceptional.

Vivek looked down his nude body, watching his penis push out of his genital slit. Deep pink, triangular, and pulsing, Vivek knew his erection would not simply retract without a release. Not this time.

Noah was corrupting Vivek's meticulous and often pious life.

Resting his forehead beside his hand gripping the bar meant to keep his arms raised while the cleanser worked, Vivek closed his eyes and pressed his other hand against his penis. A shudder of sensation went through him; it had been too long and yet he was still reluctant to do this. He immediately thought of Noah.

It was logical to assume Noah's anatomy would be different from Vivek's. Their races were both of a similar advancement from their ancient ancestors and they were genetically compatible, but that did not mean their genitalia would be anything alike. Obviously, given how Noah's clothing had tented in his lap, Noah had some type of external member that stiffened when aroused.

Vivek looked down at himself as he wrapped his fingers around his penis and stroked from thick base to pointed tip. *Perhaps Noah would be intrigued?*

He should not think like this.

But Noah had kissed him. Had, in fact, asked if Vivek wanted to kiss him, and then welcomed Vivek's exploration, moaning for more. Noah had been eager for more.

Vivek struggled to maintain his silence. He could not have Noah hear his pleasured sounds and know what Vivek did to himself. With that thought came the image of Noah not only hearing but *watching* Vivek. Would he smile to find Vivek thus engaged in pleasuring himself?

Would Noah offer to assist?

Pleasure pounded through Vivek. His heart raced and his breaths came in gasps. Wetness suddenly coated his palm, his whole body seizing with the rush of orgasm. He remained conscious of his location and tried to be quiet. Resting his arms on the bar, he braced his legs, locked his knees. For a moment, the warmth and pleasure pushed everything else away.

Something beeped. He blinked and realized the cleanser wanted to run again, clean him of his release. With a shaky hand, he reactivated it. Vivek tried to hold back his feelings of remorse and loneliness. *This* was why he did not yield to such base needs. A few moments' distraction hardly seemed worth the depressing reminder of his solitary existence afterward.

There was no male with a winsome smile and bright eyes who would pleasure him and allow himself to be pleasured in kind. Vivek had no one.

He would not indulge further. Eventually, Noah would find his place in the universe. Then Noah would no longer need him.

Vivek stopped outside the door that led into the bridge. He needed to gain access to a communications system. *Focus on your mission.*

Instead, he remembered the bright spots of pink on Noah's cheeks as he'd emerged from his cleanser compartment. The color had enhanced the blue of Noah's eyes, the dark of his hair, and the paleness of his skin. Had his flushed appearance meant he had also masturbated himself in the cleanser? Vivek had momentarily forgotten why he should resist.

Except, he had a job to do—a very important one—and fantasizing about lovely, aroused males would not save the universe from war.

A small screen beside the door activated, the captain's face appearing on it. "Yes?" he asked in Kretch.

"Captain, I would like to request access to a communications system."

"For what purpose?"

Though they may be loyalists, Vivek was not entirely certain of that. Instead of divulging that he meant to combat a shared enemy, he took another tactic close to the Krittikan heart.

"I must let my family know I was able to secure passage."

Captain Malcree grunted and nodded. "Tune your wrist link to these settings," he said as a series of numbers appeared on the screen, overlaying his face. "That will allow you to use the ship's communications system to relay your message."

Vivek smiled with genuine gratitude. "Thank you, Captain."

The screen went black, and Vivek dialed in the settings on his wrist link. Because his particular device was not typical, it would provide him with far greater encryption and packet stealth. Vivek walked away from the door to lean against a portion of the bulkhead beside a porthole. He tried to appear casual should the area be under surveillance, but his entire body thrummed with the excitement of being so near to finally completing this mission.

For appearances sake, he activated the video and played at sending an excited message to his supposed family about his success in securing passage aboard this ship. The size of the transmission would help disguise the data he would hide within it. But when he attempted to send it all, he was presented with an alert that the ship was too far out of range to relay anything more than a textual message.

Frustration battered at Vivek. They must not be near any portals or connected planets. How long would that take? He was tempted to ask the captain, but doubted it would do more than annoy him. Instead, Vivek shot off a textual version of his original message, left off the data entirely, and set his link to ping the ship's system at irregular intervals to check for a more powerful connection.

He also set a countdown that was ominously low. He did not have much time to alert the Coalition to the impending alliance of the Golson and Tev militaries.

For the first time, Vivek hoped some form of an alternative had been assigned to his mission. That if he failed, another would not. He could not now resent what he had once thought of as a lack of faith in his abilities. This was too important to risk it all with him alone.

Accepting temporary defeat, Vivek walked back toward the berth he shared with Noah and Bendel. Heat suffused him all over again at the thought of seeing Noah, being in such close proximity to him.

Should he take a tab of *alinex?* While he hated how the drug seemed to numb his emotions on the whole in its quest to repress sexual responses, perhaps it was the wisest course of action. If he did not act, Noah might not react.

With a sigh, Vivek retrieved the small blister pack from a pocket and freed one of the three remaining tabs. *Alinex* had curbed his loneliness on many a mission, but using it now when both the end and a willing partner were within reach seemed terribly wrong. Though Noah might offer himself for a variety of reasons—several of which Vivek did not wish to contemplate—a shared comfort during difficult times hardly seemed like something to stop. Bendel could chaperone them, after all.

Though Vivek knew he was rationalizing himself in

circles, he tucked the *alinex* tab back into its indentation and smoothed the seal over top of it. Placing the whole pack back into his pocket, he moved on toward the berth.

He would take his cues from Noah. If nothing else, he could offer the drug to Noah as well. Surely the Human was even more conflicted in his desires.

CHAPTER SEVENTEEN

His eyesight clearer, but not crisp like it had been yet, Noah stood near a porthole ten feet or so from their berth. With Bendel inside and possibly sleeping, Noah wanted to get a minute alone with Vivek. Not necessarily for a repeat, but to find out if he'd overstepped by "indulging" with Vivek earlier. After they'd left the cleansers, Vivek hadn't seemed able to look at him.

Movement to his left caught Noah's attention. Though blurry, he could see well enough to know it was a couple of the lion-men—Krittikan—crew members talking quietly. Both were brown and hairy with full manes of a darker shade, but one was shorter and leaner than the other. Since neither looked his way, Noah let himself stare.

Vivek had said being a different species was somehow dependent on...was it something about sexual compatibility? Children! That's what he'd said. Whether or not two races could breed. Looking now at the Krittikan over there, Noah had to wonder if they were Helokis, too. Could he be the father of kittens? He snorted a laugh. The crew members looked over at him, the overhead lights flashing green off their eyes, and Noah gazed back out the porthole.

Weird how the big cats didn't do a thing for him, but Vivek did. Noah had always liked his men smooth and athletic and a little mysterious. Vivek was definitely all that. What made Vivek not Human mattered less and less every time Noah was near him. Or maybe his curiosity about everything that might be different about Vivek had started to matter more? Noah wanted to get Vivek naked and explore every inch of his muscular, gray body.

Someone taking a long sniff beside him startled Noah into turning around. The shorter, leaner Krittikan very clearly leered up at him. Noah took a step back. The Krittikan stepped closer.

"What?" Noah said, only realizing he'd said that in English when the lion-man cocked his head. Strange how switching languages didn't take much thought. "What?" he said again, this time in Kretch.

"Would you like to rut?" he asked in a voice that sounded young. Was he a teen?

"Rut?" Noah said a moment before he realized what that meant. "I do not."

He sniffed at Noah and his leering grin stretched wider. "Your scent disagrees."

Hit on by a cocky alien kid because he'd been daydreaming about Vivek? That little snout had to be pretty sensitive to pick up on changes in Noah's body chemistry. He hadn't even gotten a semi.

"I am not interested," he said to the kid with a smile. He remembered what it was like to be young, take a chance, crash and burn.

The kid penned Noah in against the bulkhead on one side and went after his groin.

Noah batted that furred paw away. "Stop that. I am attempting to be nice, but you must stop. I am *not* interested." The formality of the language made what he said sound way too polite.

A series of quick gropes accompanied another deep inhale. "Your pheromones call to me."

"Gimme a break, you little f—"

"Rottok!"

Noah banged his head on the wall behind him. While he rubbed the spot, the ballsy hairball backed up fast.

A tall, broad lion-man said with plenty of snarl, "You would attempt to break a mate-bond, Rottok?"

Mate-bond? Noah looked at Rottok the Molester and easily recognized the kid's shock.

"I did not know." He backed up farther from Noah. "I *swear*, Father!"

Whatever it meant, Noah was going to take advantage of it. The last thing he needed was to be at the center of some kind of crew conflict, but this shit had to stop. "Yes," he said, "I have a mate-bond. A...very strong one. You should leave me...alone."

Did Kretch not have one single curse word?

Rottok gave Noah a deep bow just as Vivek appeared.

"Captain Malcree," Vivek said, "has a problem occurred?"

The captain took hold of his son's arm and hauled him away from Noah. "My apologies," he said to Noah. "I should have informed my overly-hormonal offspring of your situation."

"Situation?" Vivek said to Noah now.

Noah gestured at the kid. "Rottok over there came on a little too strong." *Because I'd been thinking about you.*

"Came on?" Vivek frowned at the backs of both Krittikan as they walked away.

"Wanted sex. With me."

Vivek narrowed his eyes and a red hue stained his cheeks. "I see," he said.

"I refused him, of course."

"Did you?"

That falsely uninterested tone added up to jealousy and possessiveness in Noah's opinion. Needing to know what Vivek was thinking, Noah got close and asked in Sowasish, "Vivek, what is a mate-bond?"

The tension left Vivek's shoulders and he straightened up with a scholarly look on his face. "Mate-bond is a universal term for the romantic connection that exists between Helokis individuals. It is easy to recognize given the usual public and...physical demonstrations...of affection." His blush brightened as he flicked his dark eyes between Noah and where the Krittikan had gone.

Noah dropped his voice. "What are the usual demonstrations?"

"Familiar touches. Close physical proximity." Vivek

cleared his throat and couldn't seem to meet Noah's eyes now. "Holding hands," he whispered.

All the things Vivek had done with Noah from the moment they entered the marketplace. And the hand-holding on the shuttle had probably clinched their relationship in the captain's mind.

Noah slid their palms together. "Like this?"

Vivek swallowed hard and said breathlessly, "Yes."

Abruptly, Vivek stalked over to their berth, tugging Noah along. But when they got inside, Vivek asked, "Where is Bendel?"

Noah peeked over his shoulder at the empty room. "He was napping in here a minute ago."

Vivek sighed wearily. "We must locate him. He—"

"He is a smart kid," Noah said and nudged Vivek into the room, closing the door behind him. "I doubt he would attempt to leave the ship or harass the crew." He rested his hand on Vivek's lower back and felt him shiver. "Perhaps he is determined to allow us privacy."

Vivek's breathing was faster, the scent sweet to Noah, but his eyes looked everywhere except at him.

"Noah, I have a medication that will diminish these feelings of arousal should you not wish to feel them," he said in a rush. "I took some earlier. It is quite safe."

Noah stepped back. "Are you not interested in—"

"If you object for any reason, despite what your body desires, the drug is available to you. I will take some as well." Vivek looked down at their hands. "Occasionally, the body wants what the mind cannot process."

Vivek was turned on and wanted him, but was

willing to chemically castrate himself if Noah wasn't interested? That was just about the sweetest thing.

"What if I do not object, and neither do you?"

Vivek finally met Noah's gaze and stepped closer. "You would consider a sexual encounter with me?"

Noah grinned. "I would."

"It would relieve a great deal of tension."

"Yes."

"You may as well know that I am also quite curious about Human physiology."

"What a coincidence. I am quite curious about Aguadite physiology."

They were finally alone and on the same sexy page.

Vivek's hand rested lightly on Noah's biceps, then squeezed. Noah tightened the muscle, resisting the pressure, and felt more than heard Vivek's sigh. He bent, and then smoothed both hands up Noah's body, stripping him of his dress. With the swell of his erection pulsing throughout his groin, Noah watched Vivek's long, slightly webbed fingers play in his chest hair. Such a strange sight, so foreign. The webbing stretched and he didn't have fingernails, but the feel of those strong hands sifting hairs and caressing muscles was amazing. When Vivek dipped down to feather along Noah's treasure trail, a low moan escaped him.

"How are your eyes?" Vivek asked.

His eyes? They were closed. He opened them. *Oh, that.*

"Imperfect," he said, still in Sowasish. "I do not mind."

"No, if we do this now, I wish for you to see perfectly."

Noah smiled and gave Vivek a lingering kiss. "Heal me," he said with all the desire he would've used to say *fuck me*.

Vivek smiled, too. "Lie down, Noah. Like before."

Noah did and he could hear Vivek lightly panting, those sable eyes flicking all over Noah's exposed skin and the bulge at his groin. Vivek rested one hand between Noah's pecs, pressed in, and slid lower until his palm rested just under Noah's last set of ribs. Noah couldn't stop the tiny undulation of his body into that light pressure. Vivek pressed down harder and closed his eyes.

"Just...be still," he whispered, his voice deeper as he leaned over him more and buried his other hand behind Noah's neck.

Noah closed his eyes, too, feeling that warmth spread up from his gut to merge with the heat in his neck. It blossomed in his head, he could feel it in his eyes, and the same thrumming arousal washed through him.

"Noah," Vivek whispered. "Never have I felt such pleasure while healing." He sucked in a breath. "How you give back to me..."

Noah opened his eyes, and then pushed up enough to press his lips to Vivek's. The healing heat faded, and Vivek moved over Noah until he was on his hands and knees above him. He did it so slowly, like he wasn't sure Noah would want him there. To prove he did, to take a little more initiative so he'd get what he wanted, Noah set his hands on Vivek's hips and pulled him down. Vivek settled on top of him, each of them straddling a thigh.

"You taste...sweet," Noah said, "like sugar."

Vivek moved back. "I apologize. I should cleanse my mouth to neutralize—"

"I *like* it, Vivek."

"Oh."

Noah soon found himself sucking on Vivek's pointy, pink tongue as they rocked together. The hardness pressed against him, Vivek's erection, didn't feel like a Human cock. Which it wouldn't, of course. Noah snaked a hand down, desperate to feel what Vivek's cock was like, but his pants were thick and concealing. "Naked," Noah said. "Get naked."

Vivek reared back and started fussing with his vest. "You as well."

Looking down at himself, Noah snorted at how he looked in his boxers and hacked-off booties. Yeah, they needed to go. Once he was naked, Noah looked up to see Vivek stared at his groin.

Vivek's gaze snapped up to Noah's face. "Your anatomy is very different."

"Yours too." Then it occurred to him, maybe this was new for both of them. "Vivek, have you ever been intimate with someone who was not Aguadite?"

Vivek shook his head briefly.

"Are you certain you want to be?"

He nodded just as slightly. "Are you? I am well aware of the possibilities amongst the races, but you have no such knowledge."

"Are you afraid I will not desire your differences?"

Vivek searched Noah's eyes for a moment, but didn't answer. Suddenly, he got up and stripped. Noah understood. He swiveled around on the bench and took off his boxers completely while he watched Vivek.

With his eyesight fully restored—maybe even better than before—Noah easily saw that Vivek did stand on his toes, that his feet were so long his heels were about two feet above the floor. His thighs were lean and delineated with muscle. At the juncture of them was a penis unlike anything Noah had seen. That was probably what had Vivek worried.

It was bright pink and triangular, more flat than cylindrical, and it pushed out from a slit in Vivek's lower belly. That explained why Noah hadn't been able to see anything when they'd changed in the cave; Vivek's cock tucked away when he wasn't aroused. Still no testicles, though. It was obvious that was a penis, clear it was hard, and Noah was... Yeah, still into this, still curious and turned on.

He reached out to touch the furled edge of Vivek's cock, near the base, and damn if it didn't reach back for him. Noah chuckled. "Are you doing that?"

Vivek shivered. "It is involuntary."

Noah stood up and stepped closer. It might be involuntary, but Vivek's cock met Noah's hand and even curled around to hold on. Vivek sucked in a breath and fisted his hands as he watched Noah touch him. The hot, delicate flesh was slick enough that Noah could slide his fingers up and down. Vivek groaned before panting, while Noah grinned with the wicked possibilities. He withdrew his hand, and Vivek made a quiet chirping noise.

"Do not be afraid," Noah said. "I want you."

Vivek relaxed, even dropping down to stand flat-footed, which made him a few inches shorter than Noah. For a moment, Noah smiled, but then Vivek touched him the same way, palm toward Noah and fingers down. His grip was loose but firm, pressing Noah's cock against his lower belly. Noah held onto Vivek's shoulder and locked his knees.

"Is it always out?" Vivek asked.

"Mmm, yes. Not always this full, though."

"Full?"

Vivek stroked slowly, and Noah moaned. When Vivek's hand stilled again, Noah huffed a laugh before saying, "I'd say take a look with that thing you do, but I'd probably come if you did it."

"Orgasm."

"Yes."

"I should like to achieve that together, Noah."

So formal... Noah took Vivek's hand away, and then kissed his palm. Vivek finally smiled. Stepping backward, holding that dark gaze, Noah found the bench and lay down again. Vivek resumed his position on top, but this time, Noah reached down to make sure their groins lined up. When Vivek eased down, settling onto Noah, Vivek's cock immediately curled around Noah's. They both gasped.

The slick, soft heat was like being inside Vivek. They flexed, and their cocks slid perfectly.

"Aw, yes," Noah said and gripped Vivek's back.

Vivek claimed Noah's mouth for a deep, wet kiss.

"I think it was inevitable," Vivek said, "that we come together this way."

He snorted and reached down to swat Vivek's ass. "Are you calling me easy?"

Vivek laughed and nudged Noah's chin up so he could kiss his throat, suck on it. Noah moaned, trailing his hands down to grab Vivek's ass. With a groan that vibrated against Noah's neck, Vivek rocked his hips faster. Noah planted his feet on the bench, undulating with him.

"Yeah, never mind. I'm a total slut for you."

Vivek lifted his head. "Slut?"

Noah groaned and thrust up, then realized it was a question because Vivek didn't understand the word. "Uh, yeah, we can work on your English later."

"I like how you speak Sowasish better anyway." He started his hips rocking again.

"Do I— Ugh... Do I say everything correctly?"

"You do." Vivek paused to groan, letting Noah see he was just as affected by the sensation of their bodies, their cocks, grinding like this. "Mostly, I enjoy...hearing my own...language...from your lips."

Noah couldn't help the whimpering noise that left him when Vivek took his mouth again. He wanted sweet words like that. He needed Vivek to care. He did.

Noah wrapped Vivek tight in his arms. Vivek lifted his head, moaning with his eyes closed, his hips grinding hard. The pressure was incredible, the slick slide getting wetter. Vivek got a fistful of Noah's hair, the sharp tug making Noah cry out. He was so close, so there. A little more... "Oh, fuck, yeah."

When Vivek's sucking lips attacked Noah's neck again, he nearly came. Damn, he loved that. Vivek's long lick from Noah's collarbone to his ear made him chuckle for how his whole body shivered.

"Noah, you taste so good."

"I do?"

"Salty. Yes."

"Mmm?"

"My planet is mostly high-salinity water." Vivek licked up Noah's throat, very slowly. Into his ear he whispered, "Noah, you taste like *home*."

Home was so far away for both of them. Noah didn't know how long Vivek had been gone from his, or even if, like Noah, he couldn't go back. That was another reason this felt so right. For the moment, they were all either of them had.

It pushed unwelcome heat up behind Noah's eyes as Vivek sighed against his neck and slowed his movements. Too emotional. He had to lighten things up.

But then he didn't need to because Vivek lifted his head to kiss Noah with a wild passion and renewed their frotting. It was desperate, hungry. Noah's fingers bit into Vivek's hip, his shoulder. They both gasped and grunted with the struggle and the pleasure.

Noah arched up into the pump of Vivek's hips. He tore his mouth free to drag in air only to whimper when Vivek went back to kissing and tasting Noah's neck. He'd be marked. *Goddamn, I wanna be marked.*

When Vivek ground down, his cock practically squeezing Noah's now, Noah felt himself tipping over the edge. Then it hit. There it was. Noah threw back his head and hollered as his whole body throbbed with release.

Vivek shuddered against Noah and groaned forever. With a whine of completion, Noah slumped against the bench, panting and flushed. He held tightly to Vivek's shuddering body, his sleek skin slippery now and a sweet scent filling the air.

Vivek stared down at him, black eyes wide and unblinking as he panted for breath.

"Beautiful, Noah."

Noah reached up to cup the back of Vivek's head. "Yes, you are."

CHAPTER EIGHTEEN

Vivek opened his eyes when the berth door sounded. He flinched when the Krittikan youth from earlier—Rottok—stood over him. *What?* Rottok held a wide-eyed Bendel against his chest. *Why are they here?* Noah lifted his head from Vivek's shoulder. They were still on the bench, resting after that exquisite release, but now... Vivek's anger spiked. "What is the meaning of—"

"Out," Rottok barked. "We are under—"

Something rocked the ship with force. Rottok stumbled, nearly dropping Bendel. Vivek and Noah both were bumped up off the bench and onto the floor.

Bendel exclaimed, "They're shooting at us!"

"We must get to the escape pod." Rottok reached for Noah's arm.

But Noah rolled away and began thrusting his legs into Vivek's pants. He removed Vivek's healer's robes from one of the thigh pockets and thrust them at him. Vivek didn't argue.

Another hit to the ship had Vivek going to his knees

as he exited the berth. Noah grasped his hand, helping him up, and they raced after Rottok. The corridor was deserted. That was all he noticed, so consumed as he was by the frenzied movement and his frantic heart rate until they were seated in the escape pod.

Which would not save them from anything.

"Why do you wait?" Noah demanded of Rottok once they were all seated in the small circular room. "Let us make our escape." He switched to English to say, "Fucking-*fuck* this fucking language!"

Vivek took Noah's hand. "We cannot escape, Noah. The—"

"*Why the fuck not?*" Noah's eyes were wide and panicked.

"Whomever attacks us," Vivek paused to swallow down his fears, "would surely fire upon the pod."

Noah's rosy skin blanched noticeably.

On Noah's other side, Bendel began to whisper in a language Vivek did not recognize. The child's tone sounded reverent. Prayer was, most likely, the only thing any of them could contribute right then.

Standing in the doorway, Rottok said, "Connect your belts. Should we—"

He cut himself off with a yelp, and then drew a long, thin sword from the metal loop at his side. His spin to face back into the corridor had him wobbling. He had to hold onto the doorframe and tugged awkwardly to free his sword.

A thin, circular blade protruded from the back of Rottok's thigh. Someone hooted loudly out in the corridor.

Vivek stood up.

Noah grabbed his wrist. "What are you doing?"

"I can assist." He covered Noah's hand with his own. "If the youth can distract our enemy, I may be able to do as I did in the dungeon and sneak in to render him unconscious."

Noah shook his head. "What if—"

Roars and the sudden clash of metal hitting metal snapped Vivek's attention to the doorway. He stepped backward to see out, to know what was happening. Noah stood and followed.

Their attacker was Tevian.

"Oh, shit," Noah whispered beside Vivek. "They followed us? Did they seriously *follow us?*"

Vivek opened his mouth, but could think of nothing to say. What other explanation could there be for a Tevian ship to be here and fire upon them? Had Solong's guards tracked the three of them to Captain Malcree's shuttle and then out here?

Why? For Noah? Bendel?

"Keep your sword *up*, Rottok!" Noah hollered.

The Krittikan lifted his sword in time to block a slash from the Tevian that might have killed him.

Their attacker said, "You are weak, child. You know nothing."

"I am *Krittikan*," Rottok said back with bite. "Do your best, and I will still win."

More laughter and a series of quick moves had Rottok clearly struggling to keep up. He was skilled, but not as good as the Tevian soldier.

Vivek advanced to again attempt to take advantage of

the diversion, however small the space in front of him. Rottok managed a twist that cut open the Tevian's sword arm.

But then the youth shouted and raised his sword in triumph.

"No!" Vivek and Noah both yelled.

The Tevian lunged forward, using the full length of its serpentine body, and speared through Rottok's abdomen.

When Vivek rushed out, Noah was beside him. They grasped the fallen Rottok by his arms and hauled him away while the Tevian paused to care for his own injury. Clearly, he felt they were no threat.

"Arrogant youth," Noah muttered even as he petted the fur around Rottok's panicked eyes. "I will speak to your father about your training as soon as possible."

Rottok shook as his red blood slicked the floor beneath him.

Vivek thrust both hands against Rottok's abdomen, framing the wound. He immediately set about investigating, healing. "You are lucky," he said. "No injuries to vital organs. You will be weakened by the blood loss, but you will survive."

"Thank you," Rottok whispered.

Vivek nodded, still knitting the torn flesh back together with the flow of energy between them.

"I can't believe," Noah said, "that they're using swords. *In space.*"

"Obviously," Vivek said, "anything else could inadvertently damage the hull." And Bedalus help them if that should happen.

Vivek pulled back his talent and smiled at Rottok's sleeping face. The youth would survive. But now Vivek would have to do his best to defend them. He had never used a sword before. He took a breath and looked to Noah.

Noah smiled menacingly into the corridor.

"Noah?"

"They should've risked the damage," he said, his voice low and deadly. He picked up Rottok's long sword and drew a shorter one from another scabbard. He stood up and slashed the air a few times with each.

He could not think to—

The Tevian bellowed, "Which of you will meet me now?"

"Noah?" Vivek stood, all else forgotten as he stared in horror.

Noah's only answer was a swift, rough kiss to Vivek's lips before he stalked out into the corridor.

CHAPTER NINETEEN

"**N**oah, stop!"

"It's all right," he said to Vivek even as he stared at his enemy's blood-thirsty, reptilian grin. "I can do this. Don't worry."

It was easy to slip into this role. He couldn't do a damn thing about a spaceship under attack except panic. But this? Fight with swords? Oh, he had this. It was finally something he could do to save himself and everyone else.

While the snake-alien's technique had been sloppy with what honest-to-god looked like an ancient falcata sword from Earth's far past. Noah knew what he'd seen. The bastard had never had to do much more to win than just show up. With a challenge? He'd fail.

Frowning, the snake-monster gestured at Noah with his sword. "What are you?" he said in that other language, the universal one Vivek had given him.

Did it really not know? Weren't they here to capture him and, maybe, Bendel? If not, then what the hell?

Fuck it. He didn't need to know right now. Instead, he embraced the chance to taunt. "Death," he said. "What do they call you?"

It hissed at him, fangs bared, and attacked. For just a moment, Noah watched, studying. But there wasn't much to see. No real training at all. A yell, rushing in, arm raised, and sword nowhere near able to protect the idiot like that...

Noah lunged with his rapier-like sword and stabbed the thing in its neck. Instead of withdrawing, he slashed sideways, opening its throat. Red blood spurted against the gunmetal wall. Its sword clanged on the floor before it grabbed at the wound, eyes wide and mouth open. It turned, lower body coiling tightly, but fell flat a moment later.

Surprise, asshole.

"Will that kill him?" Noah called behind him without looking away from the dying snake-monster.

Bendel was the one who called out, "Yes!"

Noah stepped over the twitching body. He could hear the clash of swords ahead of him.

"Stay here, okay? I'll be back."

While he walked, checking open passages and listening for anyone coming his way, Noah tried to hold onto the adrenaline and need to fight. He'd think about the life he'd taken later. Now, that was just some creature he'd had to stop from getting to Vivek and his friends. It hadn't even been Human. *Didn't matter. It was nothing.* And Noah had warned it, so...

Back near the berths, Noah found the fight he'd been hearing. Krittikan and black-scaled snakes snarled and slashed at each other, both sides showing signs of injury. Bright red blood slicked the floor and sprayed the walls.

An albino Krittikan Noah hadn't seen before was leaning against the bulkhead, clutching at his sliced chest. A large calico fought in front of him. When a second snake-monster joined in against the calico, Noah stepped up, too.

They were in this together. No longer his enemy, these lion-men were his allies against a new, shared adversary. Letting go of the past, Noah cut across the back of one snake's neck. The calico took immediate advantage of the sudden distraction to rake his serrated swords across the other attacker's chest. Both snake-things fell to the floor dead.

The calico Krittikan gave Noah a fanged smile before his eyes went wide. "Behind—"

Noah spun around and blocked an attack with the cutlass. He stabbed with the quasi-rapier, up and through. His enemy coughed blood into Noah's face, shock on his own. Noah kicked it free to die with the others.

The calico was crouched down and attempting to lift the albino. "Vivek," Noah said, "the healer, is that direction." He pointed back the way he'd come.

"My mate and I are in your debt," the calico said before lumbering off with the albino tucked close to him.

Noah spared them a small smile before he wiped his face and turned once again into the fight.

Though injuries were plentiful on both sides, it looked like the Krittikan were holding their own. Noah recognized the brown bulk of Rottok's father, the ship's captain, using a metallic glove and an axe to swipe and whack at the snake he fought. It was becoming clearer to Noah that their enemy must not have known who they were attacking. The Krittikan weren't intimidated and fought with the ferocious roars and impressive strength of the lions they resembled.

Noah helped dispatch one more snake-monster before it was all over.

He stood, swords dripping, and gulped air for a moment. His heart still pounded and his perception of everything was on high alert. Not done yet, he turned to head back, make sure Vivek and Bendel were okay.

"Noah!"

He had time to turn before Vivek was there to grasp Noah's face between his hands. "So much blood," he murmured. His eyes flicked everywhere as his breath heaved in and out.

The heat of Vivek's healing immediately seared into Noah's skin, alighting nerves already on the edge from fighting. Everything in him sang and he moaned, the sound forced out of him. "Not...mine," he managed to say. Holy shit, if Vivek didn't stop, Noah would come right here and now. He dropped both swords, and clutched Vivek's waist.

"Yes." Vivek gulped and withdrew the heat.

But Noah was already too high to resist. Without another thought, he pulled Vivek down, slamming them together. It knocked the wind out of him, but he didn't care. His lips found Vivek's and he devoured him.

Clutching at Vivek's waist and the back of his head, Noah lost himself in that sweet taste and memories of how fucking this man had felt. He wanted it back. He'd been cheated out of more and he *wanted* it.

"As athletic as this rutting may become," a dangerously low voice said, "we do not have the time to indulge. Not all of our enemy is dead."

Noah separated from Vivek, but didn't let him go. The captain stood beside them.

"Some escaped back into their ship," he continued, "and mine is disabled. We cannot allow them to detach and re-engage their weapons. We will re-arm ourselves and overtake their ship."

Noah nodded and turned to Vivek. "You should—"

"Go with you."

"No, you—"

Vivek grabbed Noah's upper arms. "Do you know what I felt as you walked away?"

Noah stared into Vivek's anguished eyes and swallowed hard before he could whisper, "I did it because I knew what to do to protect you."

Vivek took a deep breath and dropped down to be flat-footed. As he exhaled, he leaned his head on Noah's shoulder. Noah kissed Vivek's neck and held him. Everything in him sang with knowing that he meant so much to Vivek already. Noah smiled, cherishing the feeling.

"Heal the wounded," Noah whispered. "Do what you can to save us all." He moved back and cradled Vivek's face in his hands. "I'll do my part, too."

Vivek closed his eyes and sighed again. He held each of Noah's wrists and kissed his palms. Looking right into Noah's eyes, he said, "Come back to me as you are now."

Noah kissed him. "Promise."

Vivek shook his head, but smiled.

CHAPTER TWENTY

V ivek had never been so afraid for someone.

He concentrated on his Krittikan patients—for healing could not happen without concentration—but in between mending lacerations and punctures, Vivek's mind returned again and again to Noah.

All but two of the able-bodied Krittikan crew members had stormed the Tevian ship through the docking collar the soldiers had fixed to the hull. Which, he soon learned, was only four Krittikan and Noah. Vivek had watched Noah disappear inside the other ship, heard a few incoherent yells, the strike of metal, and then...nothing. He had not been able to concentrate at all then, urging one of their newly healed defenders to please look in and confirm their side had not been slaughtered. The Krittikan had looked and explained that the others had merely progressed further into the ship.

It was not a comfort.

They had not known each other long, but Vivek was more concerned for Noah's welfare now than he had ever been of his own during one of his missions. Would Noah worry for Vivek's safety were their roles reversed? Did Noah care that deeply?

And Vivek's blasted mission... Time was of the essence, and yet he was once again delayed. The two Krittikan guarding him and the wounded had speculated that the captain would relay for assistance and wait here. Vivek could *not* wait. It seemed his only course of action was to admit his true reasons for his travel, gain their sympathy, and make use of the ship's long-range communication system.

These Krittikan were loyal to their people and not their former Golson overlords. They would help him prevent Gol from allying with the Tev. He was roughly eighty percent certain they would help. Maybe eighty-five.

"Woo-wee!"

Vivek twisted around from his crouched position so fast, he spun himself onto his backside. But there was Noah, his chest covered in more blood, and...a big smile on his face.

"The ship is ours," he hollered in Kretch and held his swords over his head. Triumphant exclamations followed from the Krittikan crew.

Vivek could only focus on the blood. He dashed toward Noah.

"Rest easy," Noah said in Sowasish when Vivek was close. "Again, this blood is not mine."

Swallowing down his rush of fear and worry, Vivek waited while Noah leaned his weapons against the wall.

The long sword still had fresh blood slithering down its length.

"Come to me," Noah whispered.

The soft, knowing expression on his face and his continued use of Vivek's native language had Vivek feeling alarmingly emotional. He dove into Noah's embrace, gripping him about the shoulders as if he meant to never let go.

Aside from an alleviation of needs, Vivek had paid little attention to forming bonds in the past several cycles. Had he unconsciously bonded with Noah? The thought choked him further.

When someone called his name, Noah pulled away enough to look over. Vivek could only stare at the pale and furry profile of this Human who had him so ensnared. Worry that his feelings were not or could not be reciprocated flashed through him just as Noah looked back at him.

"What is this?" Noah whispered and frowned as he cupped Vivek's cheek. "I am well. *All* is well, in fact. None of us were injured. Please, do not worry any longer, heart of... Sweet..." He chuckled and switched to English to say, "Sweetheart. I guess Sowasish doesn't have that endearment."

Vivek smiled tentatively. "You wish to use an endearment?" The thought lightened the pressure inside him.

Noah hummed as he leaned in to brush their lips together. "You'll just have to get used to an English one."

Vivek sealed their lips, the kiss slow and deep. His worries, all of them, faded as he let the physical act express his emotions to Noah. Whatever foreign words Noah wanted to label Vivek with, he would wholeheartedly embrace them for what they meant.

But the scent of blood on Noah had Vivek withdrawing from him. "We must clean you," he said and took Noah's hand.

"I can—"

"No."

Vivek led Noah to the cleansers. It was imperative he wash all evidence of battle from him. Vivek held Noah's hand through programming the machine for the briefest of baths and no additional enhancements. Vivek would see to anything else Noah needed.

"Are you coming in with me?" Noah raised their joined hands.

Seeing no need to answer, Vivek walked into the cleanser unit. Only when the door slid shut did Vivek release Noah's hand, and only to unfasten the pants he wore. Since they were spattered with red Tevian blood, Vivek placed them, and then his own clothes, into the compartment meant to launder them.

When Vivek turned back around, he saw Noah smiling indulgently.

"I know," Vivek said. "I am aware of my behavior, but—"

Noah shook his head and stood closer. "Shh, sweetheart. It's fine."

That word. Something inside Vivek warmed to know that word was the one Noah had chosen to describe him. *A sweetness of heart?* Yes, Vivek felt that for Noah, too.

Vivek positioned them on either side of the bar where

they could rest their hands, and then held Noah's there, their fingers laced together above their heads. They had a moment of eye contact before the cleanser activated and the rush of air forced their eyes closed. Vivek's skin was almost instantly renewed, but he still thrummed with other needs. He kept his eyes closed and took deep breaths as his muscles twitched.

Noah's lips met Vivek's. *Yes.* Vivek opened for Noah's tongue, moaned at the sleek invasion. But it was suddenly not that member Vivek needed to suck. He broke the kiss, stared into Noah's blue eyes, and then dropped to his knees.

Fingers traced the curve of Vivek's head to his neck, his shoulder, while Vivek stared up into Noah's eyes. This Human meant *so much* to him. It was more than caring. Far more. The sudden emotion that slammed into him had Vivek swallowing hard and blinking back tears.

"Aw, Vivek. Come back up here."

Vivek stood, knees shaky, and leaned into Noah's tight embrace. "I have never felt so..." He swallowed again. He had no words.

"Raw," Noah said. "Vulnerable."

Nodding, Vivek hid his face against Noah's neck. He had no right to these emotions. Noah was the one separated from everything he knew, yet he stood strong. Vivek felt lost.

"I understand." Noah dipped his head and kissed Vivek's auditory opening. "But I won't apologize for what I did. They needed me, and I couldn't risk you being hurt." His arms tightened around Vivek's back and waist. "I'd do it again."

"It was a... I suppose I was proud to see you fight so well." He lifted his head, looked into those eyes. "You were brave and formidable. I simply did not realize..." He caressed Noah's fine face, the rough whiskers and smooth brow, soft hair and beguiling lips. Vivek wanted to demand they never part. That was what he wanted. But to require such when he did not know, could not ask, how Noah felt...

He kissed Noah instead. Kissed him with deep passion and all the claiming he felt inside. Hands roughly holding, massaging firm muscles, Vivek commanded and Noah acquiesced.

Vivek traced the shapes of Noah from broad shoulders and strong back to lean hips and firm rear. He stopped there and devoured Noah's mouth while his mind conjured the one act that would most definitely give Vivek the ownership he needed in this moment.

"You want inside me?" Noah asked, his lips brushing Vivek's as he spoke.

Vivek knew he should cease being surprised that Humans enjoyed similar carnal acts, but... "You do that?"

"I'll do it whatever way you like," Noah said with a grin. "I get the feeling you want to make me yours right now, though." He cocked his head. "You need to own my ass, Vivek?"

He said it as a joke, even chuckled. Noah did not realize how correct he was. Vivek *did* want to own Noah, exclusively and completely. Though he may mean it far more seriously than Noah knew, Vivek would not miss the opportunity given to him.

With a grin that felt feral on his face, Vivek urged

Noah to turn around. Noah did not hesitate to widen his stance and tip his backside upward. The immediate submission made Vivek's blood rush that much faster. Yes, *this* was what he craved.

"I need lots of lube—lubricant—and go slow to start," Noah said over his shoulder, "but I'm all yours, sweetheart."

The endearment was at odds with the cocky grin, and Vivek hesitated. His pulsing desperation abruptly dissipated. Did this mean *anything* of significance to Noah?

Noah rested his cheek on the smooth surface of the cleanser and his expression softened. He reached back, brushing Vivek's hip, and Vivek stepped closer. "Take me, Vivek," he said quietly. "I want you to."

Vivek leaned against Noah's solid form and took a deep breath against the back of Noah's neck. He shivered when Vivek sighed, and then Noah canted his hips to rub his bottom against Vivek's cock. A tremble of pleasure shook Vivek and had him pressing closer, rubbing. The need to claim returned, but without the thunderous aggression of moments earlier. Noah had said to take him, but Vivek wanted now to give.

Heeding Noah's request for lubrication, Vivek reached out and let the cleanser drop two dollops of it into his open palm. This cleanser was very well-equipped for illicit acts. He had not known the Krittikan were such physical beings. Would it not embarrass him to death, he might have thanked them for their thoughtfulness.

Noah wiggled and laughed when Vivek's attention zeroed back in on Noah's pert backside. Vivek smiled himself now as his dry hand spread the globes apart and he discovered a darkly furred crevice. "You have hair everywhere," he blurted.

"You like?"

"Oh, yes. You are so different from me."

It was a feature Vivek had not known he desired until it was presented to him. Always, his partners had been Aguadite and as hairless as he was. Now, though, while he slicked Noah's divide and searched out his nether hole, Vivek enjoyed the unusual texture. And it was apparent from his sounds that Noah did, too.

Noah stepped back and bent slightly more when Vivek discovered his opening and massaged it. The lubricant was slick as he swirled the hairs around and around that puckered muscle. Noah's moans and the way he moved with Vivek's fingers encouraged Vivek to smile. He did so enjoy giving pleasure to his partner. More than seeking his own gratification, he strove to ensure the other's—Noah's. When Vivek slipped one finger inside Noah, they both groaned.

The sight of his gray digit disappearing into Noah's pink clench sent a shudder of awareness through Vivek. He knew so little about Humans. Though Noah had proven very similar to Vivek's physiology, Vivek was uncertain whether they might enjoy the same physical sensations. Vivek watched Noah for his reactions and sought to discover whether Noah possessed the gland that would—

"Oh, fuck." Noah arched his back. "Right there. That's it."

So, yes, Human males were built the same as

Aguadite. Reveling in his discovery, Vivek added a second finger and pumped them in and out, occasionally giving the slight bump inside Noah's passage a little rub.

"I'm ready," Noah said between panting breaths. "Goddamn that was fast."

Assuming what he meant, Vivek pressed in with three fingers to test Noah's relaxation. While Vivek's cock was not long, he was thick enough at the base to warrant some cautious consideration. Noah clawed at the cleanser's wall and groaned deeply, rocking back to meet the slow plunge of Vivek's fingers inside the snug heat of his body.

"You *are* ready." Vivek removed his fingers, felt a feral delight at Noah's whine, and then spread the remaining lubricant along his cock. "As am I," he whispered as he aligned them and slowly pushed in.

Noah's breath caught, but he leaned back as well, encouraging Vivek deeper. The move and the sensation of such a heated grasp plunged Vivek back into a headspace requiring him to possess Noah. With care and attention, yes, but now and fully.

When Vivek was engulfed within Noah, he wrapped his arms around Noah's middle and pressed kisses to the back of his neck and shoulders. Noah hummed, his breathing quick as he pushed against Vivek, his need clear. Vivek undulated his hips, not thrusting, but moving enough to feel it. Noah's soft cries, the way he slid his hands up the wall, and how he moved with Vivek spoke of his pleasure more clearly than words could have.

"You are mine," Vivek said in Sowasish before he realized he had spoken.

But Noah simply agreed. "Yes," he practically hissed and covered one of Vivek's hands against his stomach.

Now Vivek panted and quickened his movements. He kept their upper bodies tightly together, but bent his knees enough to allow more upward thrust. Noah grunted with each one, his every muscle strung tight and a light sheen of salty sweat slicking his pale skin. Vivek licked and sucked, reminded again of his home waters. The rightness of this moment throbbed through him along with his building release.

Noah was soon wailing with each thrust, no longer moving with Vivek, only standing on shaky legs. Guessing Noah was close to his peak, Vivek relinquished control and pounded into Noah's willing body. The depth did not change, but the quicker pace had Noah arching his back to push himself into the cradle of Vivek's pelvis.

With a deep groan, Vivek plunged hard into Noah and stayed there as his entire body pulsed and strained. He gripped Noah tight and buried his nose in his soft hair. A moment later and Noah, too, quaked and moaned. Vivek felt the warm splash of Noah's semen on his forearm. He reached down and found Noah's hand slowly and firmly tugging on his own cock. Vivek kissed Noah's neck, licked him, and rested his hand over Noah's. Another squeezing spasm had Noah tightening on Vivek's cock still so deep inside him, and they both cried out.

Only when Noah's knees buckled did Vivek withdraw. "Easy," he whispered and was surprised by the roughness of his voice. His hands were gentle, though, as he guided Noah around to face him. "Do you need to sit?" Vivek asked.

Noah's grin was crooked, his pale face flushed a dark pink. "Could be a while before I can."

"Was I too rough?" Shame coursed through him. "I can heal you, if—"

Noah's fingertips covered Vivek's lips. "I've never had anyone fuck me like that. It was amazing. You were so deep the whole time and your cock kept doing some wiggly thing..." He trailed off to close his eyes and quietly moan.

Pride washed through Vivek now. He stepped in close and kissed Noah sweetly. Noah rested his arms over Vivek's shoulders, and it had Vivek feeling a renewal of that earlier possession. He held Noah and kissed him, for the first time in so long having no regrets in the aftermath of such needed release.

When Noah sighed and his eyelids drooped, Vivek encouraged him back to the bar and reactivated the cleanser. Noah chuckled sleepily when Vivek grasped Noah's backside and pulled his cheeks apart to ensure he would not remain slick there. Once the light and air dissipated yet again, Vivek reversed his earlier care and got Noah back into the pants, now clean as well.

Their walk to the passenger berths was unhurried and they held hands again. Noah's shoulder bumped Vivek's a few times, and it warmed Vivek to guide Noah onto the sleeping platform inside their berth. Noah rubbed at one eye as Vivek sat beside him. He could not stop watching Noah.

"Vivek?"

"Yes?" He carded Noah's hair through his fingers.

"I know it's a little late to ask this, but do I need to worry about any sexually transmitted diseases?"

Vivek frowned. "Do you have such a thing?"

"No." He shook his head. "No, I'm healthy. But...you..."

"Oh, I see." Vivek smiled reassuringly. "Aguadite have no such illnesses."

"Okay. Good." Noah grinned. "Because we're gonna do that *a lot*."

Though Noah closed his eyes and seemed not to struggle with that revelation, Vivek's heart beat faster and his breath caught for a moment. Could Noah mean to remain with him? Would he appreciate knowing Vivek wanted the same?

Uncertainty warred with Vivek's hope, so he said only, "I agree."

Noah smiled as he drifted off to sleep.

CHAPTER TWENTY-ONE

Opening his eyes, Noah realized Vivek was wrapped around him. Even sleeping, Vivek wanted to protect him. He'd never had someone so concerned about him. Was it because of what they'd been through together? Stressful situations did strip a man down to his true self. They were both open and honest now.

Noah smiled and traced Vivek's side from shoulder to thigh. Their time in the cleanser had been...everything. Vivek had been so intense. From how he took care of getting Noah cleaned up to how Vivek had fucked him deep and fast, it hadn't been like anything Noah had experienced with anyone else. He'd loved it.

He'd felt loved.

Noah cupped the back of Vivek's smooth head, and Vivek's eyes blinked open. His reflection was clear in the large obsidian eyes looking back at him. Vivek smiled sleepily. Noah kissed him.

A knock at the door startled them apart.

Noah groaned. "Again with the no morning sex."

"Technically, it is not morning." Vivek pointed to a series of numbers above the door that Noah hadn't noticed. They looked more like coordinates than a time.

"Guess I'll just follow your lead then," Noah said.

The smirk he got from Vivek held sexy promises.

"Give me a moment," came Bendel's young voice from the blanketed bundle down near their feet. "I will go to the common area."

"Oh, no, it's fine," Noah said as he blushed. He'd completely forgotten about Bendel, that he might come back to the berth. They'd quickly set it up as a big bed, and then made out and rolled around until they'd fallen asleep again. "Go back to sleep, kiddo." Noah made sure the blanket covering him and Vivek hid their nakedness.

Another knock had Vivek reaching over to slide the door open a few inches. "Yes?" he asked in Kretch.

Noah looked out and recognized the calico Krittikan standing in the hall, the one he'd helped to protect the injured albino.

"For the Warrior No-ah." He brought out clothes from behind his back, presenting them with a smile. "Captain Malcree explained that you were forced to pretend servitude to escape Tev. The ruse is no longer necessary."

Noah felt a little giddy as he leaned over Vivek to grasp the clothes. "Pants," he whispered.

Vivek laughed. "Let me assure you, he is grateful."

"Correct. Yes. Grateful," Noah said as he sat up and shook everything out.

The pants were dark brown and a lot like Vivek's

since they had pockets all down the outside of both legs. Made of some kind of stretchy fabric, they felt durable but lightweight in his hands. The shirt was a pale yellow —not the most flattering color for him—and it was billowy and laced like a sneaker from neck to hem.

"Let us dress," Vivek said, "and then we can speak with the captain."

The pointed look Vivek gave Noah had him nodding before he thanked the Krittikan again, and Vivek closed the door.

"Why do we have to speak to the captain?" Noah arched and wiggled his way into his very own pair of pants. The fabric felt silky against his bare skin. He sighed.

Vivek got his own pants on, and then tossed the blanket off of them so they could find their boots. "I must explain my mission to him and request access to the communications system. The time is approaching critical."

"For the alli—" Noah cut himself off after a glance at Bendel.

"I know of it," Bendel said while he rubbed one eye.

"How do you feel, Bendel?" Vivek asked. "Do you need another session?"

He smiled, but it looked tired. "I am well." His smile faded. "Physically."

Noah got his shirt on and crawled over to hug the kid. "Want to talk about everything that happened? Might make you feel better."

Bendel patted Noah's knee. "I do. Perhaps after your meeting with the captain?"

"Sure." Noah checked with Vivek, who nodded. "We're here for you." He rubbed his palm up and down Bendel's thin arm. "Whatever you need."

"Thank you."

They got out of the berth, and Vivek secured the sleeping platform back against the wall. Bendel dug through their bags and passed out rolled sandwiches full of what Noah assumed was vegetables and maybe some kind of cheese. He didn't ask for specifics since it tasted good. After more water from the little teapots, he put on his booties and tagged along with Vivek to find Captain Malcree.

"These clothes suit you," Vivek said with a smirk.

Noah smiled back. "Except for this footwear, I feel... purposeful," he said and liked that they spoke Sowasish to each other.

Vivek nodded thoughtfully. "To be accepted by the Krittikan as one of them is rather unusual, I believe."

"Accepted?"

"He called you 'warrior' as an honorific."

Accepted as one of these fierce lion-men? *Damn.* He'd fought beside them because he could and, well, because it was the right team to fight with. And he couldn't let them take him back to that dungeon. Couldn't let them take any of them back there.

"Vivek, do you think the snakes—the Tevians were here for me?"

He made a considering noise. "Perhaps. Or perhaps they meant to recapture Bendel. I do not know enough about their reasons for keeping either of you to— Actually that is incorrect. I was in the room when Solong demanded you be brought to him. He wanted the weapon you used on his soldiers."

Noah gulped and closed his eyes. That's what they'd wanted? The zap guns? *Shit*.

When he felt Vivek cup his cheek, Noah opened his eyes. "They cannot have you," Vivek said, his voice hard and certain.

Noah smiled. "No, they cannot." He kissed Vivek's palm.

They finished dressing, and then walked through the battle-scarred corridors.

The zap guns might've been handy here like they had been when *Swallowtail* had been attacked, but—

Ah, hell. His crew. How could he have forgotten his lost crew members? He shouldn't lose focus on them for one damn second. *For fuck's sake.*

Noah rubbed at his eyes while Vivek got directions from a Krittikan to the captain's location. For some reason he was on the other ship. Vivek didn't hesitate to go there, and Noah felt the gravity of Vivek's mission now combined with his own need to do something, anything, for Ledger and that Dunkirk guy. Were they safe? Did they have allies like he did? Christ, he hoped so.

Finally, they stood outside the bridge of the other ship, a dark gray door barring their entrance. Now that the surviving snake-men were locked in a section of the cargo hold on the other ship, did Captain Malcree own this ship? Was that why he was here?

Vivek pressed a button that resulted in a distant buzz on the other side of the door. They waited, but nothing happened. Vivek was reaching for the button again when what looked like metal claws stabbed through the tiny gap between the door and the wall. The door was shoved sideways, and there stood the captain, feline face snarling.

"Idiotic technology," Malcree grumbled. "Their language is backward as well."

They hadn't been able to open the door? Noah bit back a chuckle.

"Apologies," Vivek said, "but I must speak with you on a matter of great importance."

The captain nodded his shaggy, brown head. "Of course. Your care has been invaluable to me." He turned and gestured to where Rottok sat watching them. "My son lives thanks to your healing."

Pink colored Vivek's neck and face as he dipped his head. "It was my honor."

"Tell me what you need. You as well, Warrior No-ah."

And there it was; he'd earned a title and respect from a people who had terrified him just a few days ago. *Amazing.*

Vivek straightened his shoulders. "I need access to the communications system. Full access. There—"

"Why?"

"There is a matter of utmost urgency I must communicate to Benne Delong Songhia."

"What type of matter?"

Noah pressed his shoulder into Vivek's. He might as well tell everything. They were wasting time.

Vivek sighed. "I am an intelligence retrieval officer with the Coalition's Outer Rings division and I have information on the impending alliance between Tev and Gol."

The captain flinched. "*What?*"

Vivek nodded. "I must relay the date and location of the meeting so that Coalition forces—"

Whatever the captain said then was, apparently, not in the vocabulary Vivek had provided to Noah during his language transfer. Noah almost smiled. Swear words, probably. Lots of them. And every Krittikan head was now turned their way.

"It is impossible." Malcree held up a hand when Vivek opened his mouth. "During the initial engagement, we fired at this ship and have now discovered we disabled their communications. As ours are equally destroyed, we are entirely without the ability to request assistance or relay your message."

Vivek stared. "Shit," he said.

Noah did chuckle then because the captain cocked his head and frowned. "The situation is full of excrement," Noah translated.

The captain nodded solemnly. "Agreed. It is exceedingly shit."

An unavoidable giggle bubbled up out of Noah. He tried to hold it back, but tears came to his eyes and his whole head felt flushed. It wasn't that funny, but oh, goddamn, it was hilarious that his main contribution out here in the vastness of space was introducing two alien races to a swear word.

"And saving our lives," Bendel said from somewhere behind them.

Noah sobered with a cough, looking around to see Bendel standing at the bottom of the steps. The kid's face was pale with dark crescents under his big, brown eyes. Adopting Vivek's tactic, Noah said, "It was my honor."

"They will tell stories of your valor for generations." With that and a small smile, Bendel walked away.

Noah didn't know who Bendel's "they" might be, but like he'd told Vivek before that epic fuck, he'd had the skills to defend them, so he'd done it. He didn't feel like a hero.

Vivek cleared his throat. "Can either ship continue our journey?"

"This one can," the captain said. "Our port engine is too badly damaged." He flipped his wrist the same way an annoyed cat might flick its tail. "We were discussing our ability to tow my ship and how long it would take to reach the Benloski String."

"Not Maura?" Vivek asked.

"No. Maura does not have a space dock. Station 23 is our best option for repairs now."

While Vivek sighed, Noah just had to say, "You had difficulty opening the door. How can you pilot this ship?"

"Rottok may not be of much use elsewhere," the captain said with a grin, "but he can pilot anything." Behind him, his son beamed a smile full of fangs and pride.

Noah nodded and smiled along, but inside... *Shit*.

"What about the shuttle?" Vivek asked. "Does it have long-range communication capabilities?"

Malcree was grinning before Vivek finished. "No, it does not, but you will take it." He nodded decisively. "It will allow you faster travel and, once you are within range, you will transmit and stop the alliance."

Maybe things weren't so shitty. Noah looked to Vivek. He was smiling.

CHAPTER TWENTY-TWO

A DAMN TINY ALIEN SHIP

While Vivek went to inspect the shuttle, Noah returned to their berth. He had to know what Bendel wanted to do. Noah knew the kid was more than a kid. Bendel had a right to know what they planned. Something told Noah that Bendel was plenty capable of deciding for himself if he wanted to keep going with them.

Of course, since Noah's thoughts screamed sometimes, he wasn't surprised to have Bendel appear in the berth doorway and say, "I'm coming with you."

Bendel had already dragged their bags into the corridor and was rolling up the blankets. Noah put a hand on his shoulder and regained his attention.

"You don't have to. This could get dangerous and—"

"More dangerous than being attacked by Tevian soldiers bent on recapturing me?"

He had a point but... "Who knows. Maybe."

"I don't know these Krittikan," Bendel said. "I do know you."

"As long as you're sure, kiddo." Noah hunkered down to Bendel's height. "Thanks for trusting me. Vivek and me will get you wherever you need to go."

Bendel looked like he was going to cry, and then he suddenly lunged to hug the hell out of Noah's neck. "It'll be okay," Noah whispered and held the kid tightly. "We'll be just fine."

"I want to go home," Bendel choked out.

Noah sat back on his heels, cradling Bendel, and covered his head protectively. "That'll be our first stop then. We'll send Vivek's message, and then we'll get you home. Okay?"

Bendel sniffed, pulled away, and took a deeper breath. He squared his little shoulders and nodded. "Okay."

"Right." Noah stood up. "Let's get going." He hoisted the bags onto his shoulder.

As Noah walked away, he took a second to look back at the berth they'd all shared. He might never see it again—probably wouldn't—but it had been a good place. Laughing and learning, making love with Vivek... Not a bad set of memories for a little, golden-orange room on an alien spaceship. Noah smiled as he left it behind.

To reach the shuttle, they had to go into the cargo bay, and then climb up through the floor of the shuttle since it sat on the outside of the ship. His bad eyesight when they arrived hadn't let him see much of the interior, but now, when he stood inside the roughly six-by-eight space behind the one-man cockpit...

"Oh, shit," he whispered. He gulped back sudden

nausea and wanted to run right back down to their berth. "Oh, shit-shit-shit."

"Noah?"

He spun around to find Vivek standing in the back beside some boxes similar to the ones he'd blown up back in that cave. Noah tried to focus, but his vision was doing something weird and he couldn't breathe.

Vivek was suddenly in front of him, his hand pressed to Noah's chest. "What is wrong?" Vivek asked, all terrified concern. The pulsing heat between them told Noah that Vivek was looking for a problem inside him.

"Nothing," Noah said automatically. Stupidly. He shook his head and stepped back. "I'm fine. The shuttle's just...small."

"It is the same one we arrived on."

"Yeah, well, I couldn't see it then."

Noah tried for deeper breaths, but it sounded like he wheezed while sucking them in.

"Noah?"

"Just give me a minute, okay?"

Vivek held up his hands. "I merely wish to ascertain the cause of your current condition."

Noah huffed a laugh. "Try anxiety," he admitted. *Probably some post-traumatic stress, too*. He stared up at the ceiling and tried for deeper breaths.

"Why are you anxious?" Vivek asked in a voice like a therapist.

Noah frowned at him.

Vivek cocked his head. "Because we are leaving?"

How to explain without sounding like a pansy-ass baby?

"Honestly," Bendel said.

Noah gritted his teeth.

Vivek moved in close and caressed Noah's cheek. "Please," Vivek whispered.

The sincere concern in Vivek's eyes was easy to read. Noah ducked his head as a shiver snaked down his spine.

"I'm a dropship captain. We flew between Earth and our moon where we had a colony set up. But this wormhole got us; I don't know how. We ended up so far away that the navigation system didn't have any idea where we were. Just drifting."

He'd said that much before, but not the rest. He shivered again, harder this time. But no, he wasn't shivering, he was shaking. Trembling. He wrapped his arms around himself and closed his eyes.

"There was nothing we could do. Just...nothing. Do we burn fuel and see how far we get? What planet is that? Should we try to touch down? Is there even oxygen?" He laughed harshly, right back there in that dim cockpit staring at the screen. "*Error: Destination Lost*, the nav kept flashing that. Always goddamned lost. I was trapped on that shuttle for three...phases."

He hadn't even realized he spoke in Bedelso until not having the right word spiked anger through him. His hands shook as he raked them through his hair. "*Goddamn* it."

Vivek touched his shoulder. "But this shuttle—"

"I thought about *suicide*, Vivek."

Both of them went still, eyes wide.

He hadn't meant to say that. Another failure, piled on. He felt sick and clutched his stomach. "I need to sit."

He stumbled toward the back of the fucking tiny-ass shuttle.

Dropping onto a crate, Noah cradled his head in his hands as he leaned on his knees. Vivek's warm hand covered the nape of his neck. "Ah, Noah," he whispered. "Perhaps you should stay behind."

Noah's snapped his head up.

"No," Vivek said, "I do not wish it, howev—"

"Then no."

"The Krittikan travel to the Benloski String as well. We can reconnect once—"

"*No.*"

And that decided it. *Fuck yes.* He'd push through this useless panic to stay with Vivek. *End of story.*

Vivek nodded, his expression soft, sympathetic. "Would you like me to encourage your sleep? I can wake you when—"

"Jesus Christ, *no.*" Noah's heart beat frantically all of a sudden. "If something happens, I'm just a lump on the floor. I couldn't help, couldn't—" He gasped a breath. "I couldn't do *any*thing, and then we'd die. *Please* don't make me sleep."

"I will not," Vivek said. "It was merely an option. Rest easy...sweetheart."

Noah gulped a few breaths and nodded. Looking down, he realized he had a white-knuckled grip on both of Vivek's wrists. He let go. "Sorry."

Vivek didn't say anything, but he did lean in and gently kiss Noah. The softness of it had Noah shivering. When Vivek moved closer and wound his arms around Noah's waist, Noah held on, too. Held on tight. "I'm okay," he said, but wasn't sure who he tried to reassure.

When the shuttle's engines suddenly thundered to life, Noah and Vivek parted to stare at the cockpit. Bendel stood on the seat, bent and braced on the console, pushing buttons with his free hand. "Worry not," he said. "I can fly this model."

Vivek made a high-pitched chirping sound, his mouth dropped open and eyes wide.

"Bendel," Noah said, "what the hell? Actually, you know what? I think it's time you explained yourself. You're so not some poor, innocent kid."

Bendel guided the shuttle up from the back of the ship so smoothly it was clear he knew what he was doing. Noah watched with Vivek as Bendel tapped at the console until the shuttle swung around and the engine sounds increased. Bendel got down from the chair and stood beside it. He crossed his arms, uncrossed them, and then shrugged.

"You're right, Noah. I am not a child."

CHAPTER TWENTY-THREE

"I am eight hundred and four years old."

Vivek squinted at Bendel as Noah said, "Oh, holy fucking shit." He dropped his head onto Vivek's shoulder with a small groan.

Vivek stared at Bendel. Though he did not know of every race in the universe, Vivek had always felt confident he knew enough about most of them. He would've been taught about a race that appeared childlike when he was in training to become a healer—such a thing might contribute all manner of energy differences he would need to know.

Vivek rubbed Noah's back and asked of Bendel, "What race are you?"

"My *species* is called Pel Omdeel."

Vivek shook his head reflexively. "There are only five species."

Bendel shrugged his small shoulders. "Six."

Vivek stared. How was that possible?

"We are an ancient people, well hidden beneath the surface of Conlani." He sighed and stared out the main view screen. "I traveled back to Conlani from Benne Delong Songhia after declaring my people. Tevian forces attacked... I don't know where we were at the time. A royal guard and a member of the kier Bane royal family were escorting me." He wrapped his arms around himself.

Bendel's tale, though tragic, held fascination for Vivek as well. To think, a new species... He was uncertain of the history, but it had surely been generations since a new race had declared itself to The Coalition. Far longer since a new species did so. There would be so much to learn.

"Wait," Noah said. "There were others with you?" He pointed to the rear of the ship, his eyes wide. "Did we *leave them* in that dungeon?"

Bendel held up his hands. "No, though I wish we had." He swallowed hard and closed his eyes for a moment. "They were killed while trying to protect me."

Noah exhaled loudly as Vivek said, "Was a distress signal sent? Does anyone know?"

"I don't know." There was such weariness in Bendel's young eyes.

Noah asked, "You said somebody royal was with you."

Bendel nodded. "The kier Bane family rule the largest territory on Conlani."

"Oh, dear," Vivek said. "That has the potential for conflict."

"Shit," Noah grumbled.

Bendel walked over to Noah. "Are you very upset with me?"

With a heavy sigh, Noah looked at Bendel. "Not really. Just... It's just one more unbelievable thing piled onto a hell of a lot of them, you know?"

Bendel giggled, sounding very like the child he appeared to be. "Up to your eyeballs in crazy shit?" He wagged his finger at Noah. "I'm going to remember that one."

Noah's laugh was sudden and loud. He shook his head as he tickled Bendel's side, making him squirm away. But Noah caught him up in a hug. Their uninhibited mirth faded to sighs while they held onto each other.

Vivek already knew he had mentally adjusted to the level of knowledge and experience within the being before him. Noah, though, had not changed his regard for Bendel at all. It was rather charming to witness. Humans seemed remarkably adaptable, but here Noah did not budge. Bendel was, quite possibly, a dignitary amongst his people, but Noah saw a friend, perhaps only a child, who needed help.

A sweet heart, indeed.

"So you went to this center planet to let them know your people exist?"

Noah still sat on a crate in the back of the shuttle.

Vivek had taken one of the chairs in front of the control panel, but he was as interested in the conversation as Noah was. Bendel sat cross-legged on the floor in front of Noah, explaining all about himself and his reason for leaving Conlani.

As distractions went, it was awesome. Noah could breathe and, though his leg would bounce now and then, he was doing okay in the tiny shuttle speeding through space.

"Yes. Technically speaking, we should have done so when the Sah'dre declared themselves to the council so Conlani could enter The Coalition of Planets."

"And the Sah'dre are the people who live above ground on Conlani," Noah said, mostly to remind himself since he was learning a hell of a lot of new vocabulary words right now.

"Correct."

"So why didn't you come out then?" Noah asked.

Bendel shrugged. "We were not ready."

"Not ready? What do you have to be *ready* for?"

The look Bendel leveled on Noah right then was not something an eight-year-old could do. "Are you, at this very instant, prepared to disclose every detail of you entire race to a panel of ninety-seven judges? Will you pass the inspection that will determine—forever— whether your people are worthy of inclusion in a galactic league of protection against those who would rape, slaughter, and devastate any planet they can reach?"

Noah stared for a second, and then looked away. "No," he said quietly, "I'm not."

"Well, then." Bendel took a deep breath and blew it

out. With less pique he said, "It took us four cycles—years
—to collectively agree to declare ourselves and another
five before we felt we would not damage the membership
the Sah'dre had achieved."

"I understand." Because despite the general lack of
international conflict on Earth, it seriously did not mean
everyone could come together and agree on *anything*, let
alone whether to ask for an alliance with a bunch of alien
planets. Hell, half the people on Earth would be reeling
from learning there were actual aliens out here.

Vivek   cleared   his   throat.   "Solong's   soldiers
intercepted your ship? Unprovoked?"

"We didn't know they were there until they fired on
us." Bendel fiddled with the hem of his purple shirt. "We
tried to explain that we were peaceful and our reason for
passing through their space." He shook his head and
sighed. "They would not listen, and then I allowed my
pride to intervene."

His pride? "What do you mean?"

Bendel didn't look up. "I explained who I am. My
age, my title, my standing amongst my people... I gave
them every reason to hold us all, ransom them, and—" He
looked to Vivek. "Solong wanted the secret to my long
life. He took my blood to try and find it."

Noah watched Vivek nod and close his eyes. Was it
possible Vivek had seen that secret inside Bendel while
he'd healed him?

"Vivek? Just how much do you learn about people
when you heal them?"

Vivek stared at Noah with those sable eyes. He
smiled slightly. "I know a great deal about how your body

functions and what it needs to do so at optimum performance." He cocked his head. "I do not know," he said in Sowasish, "why you take and return such pleasure when I heal you, but I do cherish the experience."

I'm unique? Noah's face heated, but he held Vivek's gaze and smiled with him.

Bendel's sigh was a little too dreamy for Noah's comfort. He lightly kicked his little knee, but that only made the kid laugh.

"Um, so," Noah said and poked Bendel a few more times. "You were going back to Conlani, right?"

"Yes." Bendel smiled. "The Pel Omdeel have been granted entrance into the Coalition both as an independent people and as inhabitants of Conlani."

"That's—"

Suddenly, something started beeping. They all jumped, and Vivek turned in his chair to the control panel.

Heart racing, Noah watched Vivek touching things and looking really intense. Was someone following them again? Did this shuttle even have any weapons? He gave Vivek a few seconds, mind a blur or worries, but if Vivek didn't goddamn say something in—

Vivek turned around, beaming a big smile at them. "I have sent my message, and received confirmation." He sighed as he slumped back in the chair. "It is done."

"Your mission's over?" Noah rushed over and grasped Vivek's hand.

Vivek nodded. "I have relayed the information. What they do with it now is out of my control."

"Do you have to report to someone? Go somewhere?"

"I do not." Vivek caressed the back of Noah's hand with his thumb. "I am free to go wherever I wish." He cocked his head and smiled. "Where do you wish to go, Noah?"

"With you."

CHAPTER TWENTY-FOUR

This was a space station.

Noah stared out of the main screen while Bendel guided the shuttle into position to dock. Noah's mouth hung open and he couldn't seem to close it. The station was just so *massive*. It was hundreds of stories tall, wide around as...well, maybe not a planet, but a small moon at least. Antennae spiked from the top and it had arms of shuttles around the upper levels and larger ships near the bottom. Noah did a double-take when he saw one windowed section had a forest inside it.

Station 23 alone made the abandoned relic still orbiting Earth look like a child's first science project. That the could look left and right and see thirty-four other interconnected stations blew Noah's mind.

Vivek had told him that some people might be born on a station and spend their entire lives there. It was damn near incomprehensible for Noah that so many other peoples were far more advanced than humans—who arrogantly thought they were alone in the universe.

Maybe there was a way for him to help open their eyes? *Maybe.*

"Securing docking collar," a mechanical voice said over their communications system. With a thump and a hiss, the shuttle was secured to the station and a light blinked on the hatch door. Bendel stood in the chair again, this time shutting things down. When he was finished, they climbed down out of the shuttle one at a time. The docking tube let them out in a boring gray corridor.

The sounds ahead of them could've belonged to any crowded urban setting on Earth. Raised and muffled voices, incoherent loudspeaker announcements, the clatter of baggage, and thump and clack of hundreds of footsteps all came at them down the corridor. But this was definitely not Earth. The clicked, gurgled, and growled languages had Noah straining to hear any familiar word. The shape, size, color, and number of appendages of the various people had his palms sweating and his breath coming in gasps.

"Noah," Vivek whispered in Sowasish. "Be at ease. We are safe, my sweet."

Like a flipped switch, Noah paused all over and found a grin. "Your sweet?"

"Yes," Vivek said as his gray skin tinged pink. He stepped in close and threaded their fingers. "I could try another endearme—"

"I like it." Noah stood up on his toes and kissed Vivek's blushing cheek.

"You two are *adorable.*"

They looked down at Bendel beaming up at them.

"*So* cute," he said and scrunched up his shoulders, his hands folded under his chin.

Noah groaned and rolled his eyes, while Vivek chuckled.

Not letting go of Vivek's hand, Noah changed the subject as fast as he could. "What can we do for Captain Malcree and the crew?"

Vivek said, "I registered the shuttle with the docking system, so he will be able to locate it once they arrive."

Back on Earth, a disabled ship would've been global news. People would've live-streamed the search and rescue efforts all day long. Did anyone care when the space travel was potentially universe-wide?

"What about sending help out to them?" Noah asked.

Bendel pointed. "Maybe they can tell us what to do."

Across the corridor, just before they would be able to see the center atrium of the station, was a small room with a counter covered in brochures. Behind the counter stood a lean, black-furred Krittikan. If Noah had to guess, he'd say it was an old-fashioned information booth, but he couldn't read the sign above the Krittikan's head.

"So I can speak the languages, but I can't read them?"

Vivek leered at him. "I will give you the written languages. Later."

Noah flashed on exactly how that little session was going to go down. A blush bloomed on Noah's cheeks when Bendel giggled.

Physically changing the subject, Noah hustled both of them over to the booth. In Kretch he summed up what had happened to them and the current state of the two ships. After a moment of alarmed hand-fluttering, the

Krittikan calmed herself enough to alert three different departments about the situation. Noah was impressed that anyone would care, let alone act so quickly. They each thanked her for her help before walking away.

Vivek pointed toward a shop front that had swirls and dots all over it. More writing?

"I must visit the healer's den," Vivek said, "and secure a new arm band." He smiled. "Afterward, I would like to purchase something for the three of us."

"Something?"

"Something," he said with a secretive little smile.

"Okay, but can we find the hotel first?"

"No," Vivek said in Sowasish, "because once I have you there, we will not leave for some time and the band, at least, is important."

Anticipatory warmth glided through Noah.

"I will be quick," Vivek said. "Then we will explore the freshwater baths."

"Freshwater? *Real* water?"

Vivek smirked as he nodded.

That was tempting. The light and air combo he'd been using didn't quite result in the same relaxation and feel of cleanliness that actual water did. He was dying for a real bath.

Or maybe I just want to see Vivek wet.

Noah held Vivek's face in his hands and gave him a slow, lingering kiss. "Run your errands. We will wait. Return soon," he whispered in Sowasish as he ran the pad of his thumb across Vivek's kiss-damp bottom lip.

Vivek smiled lopsidedly before he took off at a trot.

Noah sat down beside Bendel on a gray bench that

felt like plastic. The view through the clear partition in front of him was incredible. Like being inside a mall with a center atrium, the curved exterior walls were covered with colorful shops or more halls—presumably to shuttle connections like the one they'd docked at. Level after level of floors ringed the station from a fake skylight showing a blue sky with puffy clouds down to a ground level with a tropical-looking collection of plants.

And the people... Fur, scales, skin, even feathers! Some people were bundled up like they were freezing, while others wore next to nothing. Noah had to wonder which ones were members of his species. That short guy who looked like lava rock? The skinny one with pink, spindly arms and legs?

But, actually, did it matter what species anyone was? Everyone seemed to get along and go about their business like the diversity was absolutely no big deal.

"You are comfortable with same-sex, public displays of affection." It wasn't a question and Bendel smiled as he said it.

"Huh? Well, yeah." Noah glanced around. "Shouldn't I be?" He hadn't even thought about it.

"Oh, no. It's simply that the last time I was on Earth, they were still struggling with acceptance of the many Human differences. Changing laws, but slowly."

Noah dug back through his memories for an old history lesson on world equality and— "That was, like, two hundred years ago!"

Bendel only grinned.

Noah shook his head. "I'm not even going to ask what

you were doing visiting Earth, let alone why you knew about any laws."

"Nothing nefarious."

"Like you could be nefarious," Noah said on a chuckle.

Bendel looked out over the people and swung his legs —reinforcing his childlike appearance, though Noah doubted Bendel meant to at this point.

"So," Bendel said, "what will you do now?"

Fuck Vivek's brains out for the next week.

Bendel snorted. Noah winced a little, but— "Well," he said, "at least when my thoughts scream at you, I won't feel like I'm corrupting a minor."

"I have three wives and two husbands."

Noah did a slow pan to look down at Bendel beside him. "Excuse me?"

"Eighteen children, twelve grandchildren, and four great-grandchildren."

Rubbing at his eyes, Noah sighed. "Remind me to tell you about *Alice in Wonderland* someday. It's a lot like how it feels knowing you."

Bendel sat up and smiled. "Oh, I know it!" He looked sheepish when Noah gaped at him. "I have a particular fascination for literature."

"Unbelievable," Noah said with a shake of his head.

As they sat in silence, though, Noah's mind puzzled over that question. What *did* he want to do now? *Stay with Vivek.* He looked down at his hands resting in his lap. He didn't have to think much about that want, but was it really possible? Vivek was delivering two lost souls to a safe place and accomplishing his mission. Technically, both were finished.

When Noah had told Vivek he wanted to go with him, Vivek had smiled and pulled him down for a kiss. Noah wasn't sure what it meant to follow Vivek wherever he went now, but he knew he genuinely liked Vivek, trusted him, and knew he could rely on him. He appreciated the fact Vivek could fight when he had to, healed unselfishly, and worried about Noah. Vivek was caring and patient and—

Oh wow. Was he *in love* with Vivek?

"Of course you are," Bendel said, and then asked, "What did you purchase?"

Noah started when he realized Vivek was standing beside him. He looked up into those obsidian eyes and... smiled. Yeah, he really was in love with Vivek.

Cocking his head, Vivek gave him a curious look. "Are you well?"

"Yes. Hello."

Vivek chuckled at Noah as he sat down beside him. "Hello."

Noah's hand found its way to resting on Vivek's thigh and he got a quick kiss. Something warm and happy lit up inside Noah. *Happy*. Yeah, he was honestly and sincerely blissful and content right here with Vivek. He sighed with the feeling.

Bendel came around to stand in front of their knees and tapped the box Vivek held. "What is this?" he asked, sounding excited. "Is it something fun?"

"I suppose it could be something fun, yes." He opened the box and took out a golden band, like a bracelet. "This is a wrist link," he said, looking at Noah. "It allows the wearer to communicate with others wearing them as well as to computers like the ones on ships and shuttles. Would you like to wear it?"

It wasn't a wedding band, but it felt like one given his thoughts as Noah held out his left wrist. Vivek smiled as he snapped it on him. The band was cool against his skin and fit comfortably. Then Vivek took out another one and snapped it to his own wrist.

"Press the green jewel and say my name into it," Vivek said, and Noah did so. Then Vivek tapped his wrist link to Noah's and both their green jewels flashed. "Now they are programmed so that when you press the red jewel and say my name your link will tap my link so we can talk to each other regardless of where we are."

"They work even across the universe," Bendel said excitedly. "All you need are enough relay points between you."

Before Noah could ask if Bendel had one before his capture or wanted to get a new one, Vivek pulled another band, a smaller one, from the box. Bendel gasped, so did Noah, and Vivek handed it to Bendel with a smile.

"I believe there is a way for you to program it remotely," Vivek said, "to enable you to communicate with your family on Conlani. Or perhaps there is an embassy in one of the stations that can assist you."

Bendel pet his link, sniffed, and then pushed himself up to grab both Vivek and Noah by their necks and hug them tightly. "Thank you. Thank you both *so much*."

Noah gripped Vivek's hand and hugged Bendel. His eyes suddenly burned and he had to sniff as something tightened in his chest. He had a family. When Bendel released them, Noah turned and kissed Vivek, trying to put all his emotions into the act. He felt Vivek's surprise, but that melted into kissing Noah back. When they parted, Noah could smile.

Vivek cupped Noah's face, smiling back.

He cares. Noah was certain of that.

When Noah slid his hand over Vivek's shoulder and down to his biceps, he discovered a shiny silver band circling his muscles. Noah slid his hand over it. There was something sexy about the pliable, smooth skin and the hard, immovable metal.

"Why did you need this?" Noah asked.

"It designates the level of my abilities as an Aguadite Healer. Some are frightened by such things." Vivek shrugged. "The Coalition mandates that we reveal ourselves."

"Because of how powerful you are?"

"Yes."

Noah traced the ring with a fingertip. For some reason, he really wanted to use his tongue. He licked his lips instead. "I'm not afraid."

"Wow," Bendel said, stepping back. "Go make use of a hotel room. I will find the Conlani embassy and send word when I do."

Noah cleared his throat and tried to rein himself in. "No, it's fine. We can go with you."

Bendel huffed an impatient breath. "At this age, I am no longer able to fully appreciate the pheromones the two of you are emitting. So shoo."

Noah did his best not to grin. Apparently, being eight hundred had some disadvantages.

Bendel gave him a cute little glare before stalking away into the crowd. For a moment, Noah worried about the kid. The not-a-kid. Who maybe hadn't left his planet for a few hundred years? Did he really know—

Noah's new wrist link vibrated. *I'm fine*, appeared on the tiny screen. Noah chuckled and asked Vivek to show him how to reply.

Then they did walk off in search of a hotel.

CHAPTER TWENTY-FIVE

The only reason Vivek was not exploring the inside of Noah's mouth with his tongue was the fact there were security cameras installed in each of the lift's six corners. But Noah stood against one wall and stared at him with a look that smoldered. Temptation burned inside Vivek's chest, groin, throbbing to the beat of his heart.

They were free this time. No worries, no distractions. Safe after so long.

He would be slow. Thorough. Afterward, they would be weak with sated desires, and able to luxuriate in their combined release.

No. In their love.

He knew that was the emotion leading him down the spartan corridor in Noah's wake. Knew it now. Once everything else faded away, and Vivek could focus on the present, he understood his protectiveness and desire for Noah ran far deeper than any sense of duty or physical lust.

He was simply uncertain if Humans embraced chemically induced pair-bonding. If Noah could form a true mate-bond with him.

Ahead, Noah laughed. "I know she said room eighty-two and that my handprint would get us inside." He spread his arms and grinned. "But I still can't read the numbers."

Vivek stepped up close to Noah and felt a thrill for how he towered over him. Noah's eyelids fluttered closed as he tipped his head back, his mouth open and breath coming faster. A pink flush stole over his throat and into his cheeks. Yes, Vivek enjoyed Noah's submission.

Vivek turned Noah around with hands on his shoulders, and then guided him toward the appropriate door. He pressed his cheek to Noah's and pointed. "Eight. Two," he said, indicating each number.

Instead of pressing his hand to the panel, Noah placed both hands on the door, widened his stance, and bowed his back to nudge his backside against Vivek's upper thighs. With a slow lick up the slightly salty expanse of Noah's neck, Vivek dropped down flat-footed and ground his expanding erection against Noah's firm bottom. Noah panted, and Vivek moaned.

Enough. He grabbed Noah's wrist and flattened his palm against the access panel. *More.*

They entered the room in a frenzy of clothing flung, dropped or kicked off, and were in each other's arms, mouths devouring, in mere moments. But when they broke for a breath, panting at each other, Noah gave him such an open look of affection and caressed the side of his face so softly that the torrent of need slowed inside Vivek.

He took Noah's hand, leading him to the silver-sheeted bed.

Noah got up and positioned himself on his back, one leg bent and leaning back on his elbows. Vivek's breath caught, making him have to clear his throat before he could order the computer to lower the lighting by half. He stood there admiring the shadows cast over cobbled abdominal muscles and all that dark hair.

Noah grinned at him. "Do we have lubricant?"

Vivek pointed behind Noah at the shelf built into the bed frame. There were several complimentary necessities, including a bottle Noah should recognize. He did, picking it up to examine it before putting it back. Then he reached for Vivek.

Vivek crawled up the bed, moving over Noah, watching his skin flush and the way he licked those pink lips. He settled slowly over top of him, glad when Noah wrapped him in his arms and held tightly.

"I want you."

"I know."

Vivek let Noah have a little more of his weight and smiled when he moaned and lifted one leg to hold Vivek's thigh with his calf. Slowly, he moved his hips against Noah, not really rubbing so much as rhythmically pressing down, hard erection to hard erection. Those blue eyes watched him as Noah's breathing increased. There was that expression again. Noah held nothing back.

That this male could be so free here with him now...

"You are a wonder to me," Vivek whispered to him. He gently touched Noah's face, tracing an eyebrow, the arch of his cheek, the impossibly soft skin beneath an eye that did not blink. "You have been through so much and yet you have not broken. You are still so strong."

A little smile picked up those lips. "I did break."

"No, that was not breaking. You let some of the old go so you could embrace the new."

He ran his fingertip from the top of Noah's jaw near his ear all the way down to his chin, the stubble of his beard rasping against his skin. The contrast of it to the soft, plump flesh of his bottom lip made Vivek shiver with desire.

"I should shave."

"Never."

Noah tipped his chin down and captured Vivek's finger between his lips. Watching them close around him, pink wrapping gray, was beautifully erotic. Noah stared boldly into Vivek's eyes and sucked, his cheeks hollowing, before his tongue did wicked things in there.

"You have a word for it," Vivek whispered, "but are you interested in performing fellatio on me?"

Noah smiled around Vivek's finger. He slid free, smiling as well, so he could hear Noah's answer.

"How do you want me?"

Though it was his favorite, Vivek knew he would not be able to stay on his feet while Noah knelt for him. "I will sit on the edge of the bed, if you would be so good as to kneel beside it."

A laugh huffed out of Noah. "Deal."

Vivek removed himself from atop Noah, and Noah got down on the floor. Vivek shivered almost violently when Noah moved in between Vivek's spread thighs without hesitation, his expression hungry for Vivek's body. Noah's deep chuckle made Vivek feel flushed.

The wonder on Noah's face pleased Vivek so much. Despite their vast differences, Noah's curiosity and easy acceptance meant everything to Vivek. He hoped his own reactions to Noah did the same for him.

"Oh, hey. It's right up front, huh?" Noah ran the tip of his finger around Vivek's nether hole.

The sensation made him catch his breath for a moment. "Yes. I have what you call a prostate as well."

Noah chuckled. "Maybe I should find it."

"Please, Noah," he said breathlessly.

Noah leaned in and licked from the bottom of his hole to the tip of his penis. Chittering noises erupted from Vivek's throat involuntarily.

"You have got to be related to dolphins."

"Dolphins?"

"Let's see what other noises you can make."

Vivek's attempt to compare the definition of dolphins to his genetic ancestors was cut short when Noah swallowed every last inch of Vivek's erection. Vivek was not silent then as he buried his fingers in the soft, dark curls on Noah's clever head. Enough brain function remained in him that, when he fell back, Vivek managed to keep his gaze on Noah and see how his penis stretched Noah's mouth wide. It might not be comfortable for Noah, but there was such a look of bliss on his face that Vivek believed Noah thrived on doing this for him.

"Beautiful. Exquisite. Oh, *Noah*." That last because Noah used his tongue to play along the underside of

Vivek's penis, shooting sparks of pleasure all through him.

Noah took him inside his mouth again and sucked so perfectly, Vivek felt his climax roaring rapidly nearer. Were they so connected now that Noah knew exactly how to play him for maximum pleasure? When Noah quickly rubbed his thumb back and forth across Vivek's hole, he was certain of Noah's genius.

Back bowed and head thrown back, Vivek's orgasm crashed through him. His cries were cut off by the tension in his entire body as he burned hot and fast. The sudden intensity passed, leaving him to collapse, gasping, and twitch with sparks of pleasure as Noah continued to lick and touch him.

"Guess I'll have to go looking for your prostate next time."

Vivek meant to laugh, but a whine came out instead. "Do it now."

"What? Are you sure?"

"Did you orgasm?" Vivek looked down his sated body as Noah stood up.

"No, but won't it be uncomfortable for you?"

Noah held the base of his erection and stared at Vivek's groin, but his concern was clear. Vivek made a mental note that he should cease stimulation once Noah orgasmed.

"I will enjoy your body inside mine." Vivek shivered with the thought. "On the shelf there," he said and pointed. "Get the white oil."

Noah quickly did so, and then spilled quite a lot on his hand before getting it to his penis. The sight of Noah stroking himself slick had Vivek licking his lips. Next time he would taste Noah.

"Do you need me to stretch you or...anything?"

Vivek reached for Noah. "I enjoy the sensation. Come into me, sweetheart."

Noah smiled and got on the bed so he straddled Vivek's thighs. Watching himself, Noah lined up the bulbous, red cap of his penis with Vivek's hole. As he pushed for entrance, Noah looked up to lock gazes with Vivek. His consideration was as perfect as the pressure and burn of letting him in.

"More, Noah. Fill me."

Noah's moan vibrated into Vivek, forcing an answering noise from him. The cylindrical shape of Noah's penis was perfect for where it was. The girth and length had Vivek certain he was ruined for any other male. None would ever make him feel like this. When Noah's belly was pressed to Vivek's, Noah seated so deep inside him, Vivek realized his erection had returned in the wake of such pleasure.

Vivek thrust up, and Noah began to move.

It was fast, frenzied, and Vivek found himself crying out and scrabbling to hold Noah closer. Noah bared his blunt teeth, neck muscles straining, and skin turning deep pink. As another orgasm ran rampant through Vivek, Noah hollered, trembled, and buried himself within Vivek's spasming body.

They shook and gasped, holding tight to each other for several counts. Vivek felt shocked, overwhelmed, but also desperately content. And *connected*. So very connected in a way that transcended the physical.

Noah was smiling when he managed to lift his head. Vivek leaned up and kissed that satisfied smirk.

Eventually, Noah eased away, pulling his softened member free of Vivek's still-grasping body. He did not seem pained, so Vivek merely turned on his side and enveloped Noah in his arms. Noah sighed and pressed in closer.

"Vivek, I—" Noah exhaled hard against Vivek's skin. "Vivek, I'm falling in love with you."

Vivek lifted his head with a jerk, astounded that Noah felt the same as he did. Noah, though, had his eyes closed tightly, grimacing. Vivek watched Noah swallow hard and understood that it was possible Noah feared it was Vivek who did not share this feeling.

"Good," he said, caressing that worried face.

Noah's blue eyes blinked open, his surprise clear.

"I wish you to feel back for me what I feel for you, Noah." He threaded his fingers through Noah's thick, black hair and rubbed his thumb on his scratchy jaw. "I grow more desperate to keep you each time you are near me."

That expression of total honesty settled back into Noah's face, softening what had tensed and turning his blue eyes liquid. Vivek cared not if he ever swam in the waters of Aguada again, so long as he could bask in the heat of Noah's eyes forever.

CHAPTER TWENTY-SIX

Noah floated under the surface of actual warm water, marveling at the athletic grace of Vivek swimming. He undulated his whole body instead of kicking and, with his arms by his sides, he almost—*almost*—looked like the dolphins of Earth.

And Vivek had confirmed that, though they'd called them agolishes, what Vivek understood of dolphins seemed very like his ancestors.

Noah had been fascinated as a kid when he'd swum with a dolphin, and it was no different now.

Well, no, it was pretty different since Vivek caught him up, took him to the surface, and kissed him breathless. That was definitely an improvement over Noah's childhood memory.

Vivek bracketed Noah's body against the side of the pool, but it was like being held against a marshmallow. The whole room they'd rented was like being inside a puff. He couldn't quite decide if it was white or a really pale blue. Purple. Gray? Anyway, it was softly lit, decadently fluffy, and they'd ordered a giant indentation filled with tropically warm water.

"Noah?"

"Hmm?"

Vivek flashed his sharp, little teeth. "It is morning."

While Noah tried to figure out what he meant, Vivek ducked beneath the surface. Noah hollered in sudden pleasure when Vivek took Noah's cock deep into his mouth. Bracing his arms along the pool edge, Noah let his head fall back as Vivek sucked him. Tongued his slit. Fondled his balls. Grabbed his ass and—

"Wha—" Noah hollered as Vivek surged up, taking Noah right out of the water. In a second, Noah landed on his back, his legs still dangling in the pool. He glared down at Vivek. "What in the hell are—*oh fuck yes.*" Vivek sucked Noah's cock down his throat and stuck a blunt finger up his ass. "That's it. Yeah. *Yeah.*"

Noah's back arched and he might've slapped a hand on Vivek's sleek head as he came. The intensity of it had Noah's body jerking a few times. Was the room suddenly sparkling? He chuckled at himself as he went boneless, unable to do anything but gasp each breath.

With a splash, Vivek landed on hands and knees over Noah. "You taste like the ocean," he said, his voice deep and raspy.

"You're welcome."

"This room is awesome," Noah said as he lounged. He'd wanted something to lay back on, and Vivek had done some tapping on a screen embedded in the wall to make a form-fitting chaise push up out of the floor underneath him. "How long can we stay here?"

"A few more...hours." Another lounge chair poofed up beside Noah, but this one had an appendage. "Would you mind if I watched a few news updates?"

"News? Yeah, that's fine."

The appendage turned into a small view screen, and Noah got one, too.

Vivek gave Noah a slim disc and taught him how to control a news broadcast system. Noah settled back and watched and listened to a host of aliens speaking that common language—Bedelso—while they reported on everything from celebrity gossip to the different holidays happening across the universe to politics he had no hope of understanding.

Vivek pressed a button on the disc Noah held, changing the broadcast. A creature that looked like a talking rock was saying in a guttural voice "...announced today that a Ring Ten planet called Tev has been invited by the High Council to join The Coalition of Planets. This unexpected news comes after inside sources dispelled a rumor that Gol had been attempting to rebuild their empire twelve cycles after their defeat by Coalition forces by recruiting the citizens of Tev. Instead, Tev's monarchy has confirmed the dispatch of a delegation to Benne Delong Songhia. Confidence of an acceptance is high."

Noah took his earpiece out. "I know Tev is where we met, but I don't understand the rest."

"It means that Tev will be held to higher standards

once they join The Coalition. They will not be able to ally with Gol, and will be forced to undergo a series of evaluations to align their governmental practices with Coalition ethics." Vivek's grin was triumphant.

"And you did that." Noah smiled with him. *He's a hero.*

Vivek shrugged. "I played a part. They must have had several different plans prepared for various contingencies. The definitive timing and location of the alliance negotiations could have helped launch one of those plans." Vivek's expression changed to one of mischievous delight. "And it is possible The Coalition may find a way to move someone they approve of onto the throne."

It sounded to Noah like a coup was about to show up on that slithering bastard's doorstep. Maybe it already had. Noah leaned in and kissed the evil smile curling Vivek's lips. "Thank you," he whispered.

Vivek's cheeks turned pink as he shrugged. Then, suddenly, his attention snapped back to his own broadcast. On the display were...Humans.

"Vivek?"

Noah took his earpiece out and turned off his broadcast, while Vivek switched on the audio from his.

"...the Earth Campaign in their goal to eliminate the abduction and sale of Humans to various unsavory parties throughout the universe. As an uninitiated planet, Earth is meant to be off-limits, but the designation is often ignored by smugglers and slavers."

"Oh, shit." Noah looked away and even covered his

eyes when the display showed a pile of dead people—dead *Humans*—with pieces missing from their bodies.

"Apologies, Noah." The reporter stopped talking. "That was not the part I wished you to know."

Both their displays now off, Noah turned toward Vivek and let his hand be held. "What did you want me to know?"

"The Earth Campaign has been granted permission to patrol your solar system." He smiled a little. "They must keep their distance from your investigative devices exploring the same area, but at least this will allow them to discourage and, possibly, to prevent the abductions."

Noah ran fingers through his hair and laughed with the fucked-up-ness of that. "People really are being abducted."

"Yes," Vivek said, though he didn't need to confirm it. "This will... Oh, Noah." Vivek stood, looking frantic.

"What's wrong?"

"I should have thought of this sooner," Vivek said and lunged toward a blank wall.

Noah stood. "Thought of what?"

Vivek touched his hand to what looked like a smudge, and a large rectangular display clicked on while a keyboard popped out.

"I can register you with The Coalition's refugee program," Vivek said and started typing. "You will have to speak with someone eventually, but you are entitled to benefits that will help you establish your life here."

"Here on this station?"

"Anywhere in The Coalition."

Holy shit. He could— "Wait. Could my crew be listed in there?"

Vivek paused and stared at Noah for a moment, dark eyes wide. "Forgive me again, Noah." He turned back to the wall and did something to split the screen into two. "Spell their names for me. I will translate."

"There's nothing to forgive you for." Noah went over to him and kissed his shoulder. "We have been kinda busy."

Vivek chuckled and leaned down to peck Noah's cheek. Noah told him how to spell Charles Dunkirk's name, and then watched as Vivek typed.

Vivek shook his head. "He is not listed."

"Try Charlie."

Vivek did, but the screen didn't change.

Noah closed his eyes for a moment. Hadn't he predicted Charlie wouldn't make it?

"It means only that he is not registered," Vivek offered.

Noah nodded, though didn't hold out a lot of hope. He rested his hand on Vivek's shoulder. "Try Ledger Atwater." He spelled it all out as Vivek pecked at the keys.

This time the screen was full of information. "He is on Conlani."

"What?" Noah stared at the gibberish on the screen. "You found him?"

"Ledger Atwater registered as a refugee two turns ago on Conlani. Two days ago, that is."

Vivek touched the screen. A photo of Ledger appeared.

"That's him! That's really him." Noah's hands fluttered as he looked around. "Where's that thing you got me? I need to tell Bendel. We have to go to Conlani *now*. Holy fucking shit."

"Noah," Vivek said softly and caught Noah's shoulders. "I connected your account with Ledger Atwater's. He will receive notice of that soon, and the two of you may make contact via your wrist links."

Taking deep breaths, Noah closed his eyes and nodded. "Okay. Thank you."

Noah felt Vivek kiss his forehead. He opened his eyes and recognized the affection in the obsidian eyes gazing back at him. "Sorry I keep freaking out."

"Freaking out?"

"Overreacting?"

Vivek shook his head. "Your reactions are your own. I would not presume to understand what you have gone through or will experience going forward." He kissed Noah slowly. "I would like to be there for you."

"I want you with me."

Another tender kiss. "I will not be parted from you, Noah. I am committed."

"Good. Me, too." Noah grinned and turned to the door. "So let's find Bendel and get going. Oh, hey, can we book passage on a big ship? Like bigger than Malcree's? We'll need two room this time, too. I'll be getting that morning sex this time around. Morning, afternoon, and all night long, thank you very—"

"Noah."

"Huh?" He turned around to see Vivek holding up their clothes.

"Perhaps we should dress first."

Noah snorted a laugh. "Yeah," he said. "Yeah, that's a good place to start."

Taking his pants, Noah smiled at his...boyfriend? Lover. *Ah*. His mate. They were really mate-bonded now. And though one mission was over, they had another that they would accomplish now.

Together.

PLEASE REVIEW

Thank you for reading *Healing Touch*. I hope you enjoyed this novel.

If you have a moment, please review *Healing Touch* at the store where you bought it. Help other gay romance readers and tell them why you enjoyed this book.

Revisit the Destination Lost world by picking up a copy of *Forever Home*, Ledger's story, and *Warrior Mine*, Charlie's story. Noah and Vivek have important roles to play in both books as Noah's determination to find his crew mates continues.

Thank you again, dear reader!

ABOUT THE AUTHOR

Missy Welsh wrote and published 21 gay romance short stories, novellas, and novels between 2010 and her retirement in 2020. She lives in Northeast Ohio and paints landscapes in her spare time.

ALSO BY MISSY WELSH

Destination Lost Series

Healing Touch

Forever Home

Warrior Mine

Self-Discovery Series

Your Biggest Fan

Have You Seen Me?

Isherwood Pack Series

Yours Forever

Isherwood

SubDominant

TripleMate

Colkirk

My Summer of Wes

Just Wait

A Husband for Santa Claus

Take Your Pick

Hope Is Good

Come Cuddle Me

KLT23

Jenner's Needs

What

Made in United States
Orlando, FL
16 July 2022